BY THE WATERS OF BABYLON

A CAPTIVE'S SONG - PSALM 137

MESU ANDREWS

BY THE WATERS OF BABYLON

A Captive's Song - Psalm 137

Copyright © 2018 by Mesu Andrews

ISBN: 9781732443617

ASIN: B07D62FD5S

Published by McPherson Publishing

Sparta, WI, USA

Cover design by Josh Meyer Photography and Design

Edited by Hanemann Editorial

PUBLISHER'S NOTE

The Psalm Series is a collection of creative fiction based on the Psalms. These stories are not meant to add to or replace Scripture, but to explore the deep meaning woven through the Psalms, and to enrich our experience of the timeless truths these ancient songs of praise contain.

This particular story, *By the Waters of Babylon*, is a historical novel based on the events recorded in Psalm 137 and the Old Testament prophetic books whose prophecies intertwined with the events of Psalm 137.

For an explanation of the author's approach to the biblical text, be sure to read the Author's Note at the end of the book. And be sure to read through the Bible Study of Psalm 137, as well.

In the meantime, we hope you enjoy reading passionate poetry made into heart-pounding fiction!

For a FREE 7-Day Psalm Series Devotional, and to find the other books in the series, go to **psalmseries.com**.

NOTE TO READERS

I believe to my deepest core that my God is good, just, and righteous in all He does. He's the same loving Father in the Old Testament that gave up His Son for my sins in the New Testament. However, I find His Old Testament judgment hard to read, don't you? No matter what I know to be true about His goodness, justice, and rightness, the torturous loss of life seems harsh and cruel.

The research and writing of *By the Waters of Babylon* has changed me. Though in some places it reflects the violence of Jerusalem's captivity—portrayed as tactfully as possible—I have seen through Merari's journey the loving provision of Yahweh on the other side of His judgment. Those difficult passages of God's wrath and Judah's suffering still pull at my heart, but now I know with firm assurance that every faithful child of God was met—in captivity or in heaven—by the promise of a new and better way. Because they saw God as true to His Word, in both reward and discipline, as every good parent should be.

My prayer for you, dear reader, is that you also recognize the loving Father amid the discipline and reap its eternal fruit.

PART I

"*Along the banks of Babylon's rivers we sat as exiles, mourning our captivity,*
and wept with great love for Zion.
Our music and mirth were no longer heard, only sadness.
We hung up our harps on the willow trees.
Our captors tormented us, saying, "Make music for us and
sing one of your happy Zion-songs!"
But how could we sing the song of the Lord
in this foreign wilderness?
May my hands never make music again
if I ever forget you, O Jerusalem.
May I never be able to sing again if I fail to honor Jerusalem
supremely!
And Lord, may you never forget
what the sons of Edom did to us, saying,
"Let's raze the city of Jerusalem and burn it to the ground!"

Listen, O Babylon, you evil destroyer!
The one who destroys you will be rewarded above all others.
You will be repaid for what you've done to us.
Great honor will come to those who destroy you and your future,
by smashing your infants against the rubble of your own
destruction."
-Psalm 137

PROLOGUE

I once was a goddess who led a prince to Yahweh. Now, I'm an exile living out my life in Babylon, knowing Yahweh's words will be fulfilled. Thousands of Jews —as we are now called—have grown strong in Babylon. Someday we'll return to Judah. Yahweh promised. Jeremiah told us. "Seventy years," he said, and Jerusalem would be rebuilt.

I heard him say it, but I also saw the walls fall down. Doubt shadowed my heart for years. My journey hasn't been an easy one. I tell you my story now, how life can feel hopeless, a heart embittered, but God . . .

Yes, with those two little words, all hope was restored. *But God . . .*

For we who believed, those words mended broken hearts, turned the tide. Lives were changed. Wanderers found purpose. Those who loved much, lost much. Yet we who trusted Yahweh, allowed Him to step into the void and fill our emptiness.

Only Yahweh chooses a broken woman to heal a wounded man. Only Yahweh uses a pagan prince to offer truth to a foreign empire. And only Yahweh can use my story to change your life.

You may think change impossible—*but God* . . .

CHAPTER 1

MERARI, JERUSALEM - 588 BC

"In the ninth year of Zedekiah king of Judah, in the tenth month,
Nebuchadnezzar king of Babylon marched against Jerusalem with
his whole army
and laid siege to it."
-Jeremiah 39:1

*T*he strings of my harp felt like rods of iron in the cold mix of sleet and rain, while I played David's Shepherd Song in Jerusalem's empty streets. Eyes closed, my mind wandered through the valley of the shadow of death. How would I feed my sister and my son if I couldn't sell my harps? King Zedekiah's royal prophets had proven false and my husband's cousin, Jeremiah, had been mournfully accurate. Babylon laid siege to our city two weeks ago, and even the elite here in the upper city bought only food in the market.

You couldn't eat a harp.

But I could at least provide a measure of peace and joy. Swaying to the gentle rhythm of my music, I opened my eyes and noticed the sandal-maker's wife packing up her wares. We were the only two merchants brave enough—or insane enough —to keep our booths open when both weather and Babylon threatened. I hadn't sold a harp in six months, but I'd rather be here than fighting with my sister at home.

A trumpet blew. Then another. The ground beneath me shook with the thunder of horses' hooves. The sandal-maker's wife and I exchanged a fearful glance, and she ran toward her home around the corner without a good-bye. More trumpets sounded, and now rams' horns joined them from atop the walls around our city. The market began to fill with noblemen and soldiers, rushing past me on their way to the palace.

One man took his time, strolling past my booth with eyes as hungry as a jackal. "Your cousin Jeremiah has proven to be a false prophet, little Merari. Did you hear? The Babylonians are withdrawing. The siege is over as the other prophets said." Jehukal, the chief of forced labor, peered down at me over a rotund middle, wiping sweat from his brow on a wintry day. "But I could speak in Jeremiah's favor if you agree to meet me after the council meeting."

I smiled sweetly, suppressing a shudder, still strumming my harp. "I'm honored by your persistence, my lord, but as I've mentioned before, my son requires my attention at home." I stilled my harp and hoped to glean information to share with my husband's cousin—my cousin. "Have all of Nebuchadnez-zar's armies withdrawn or only some?"

"Changing the subject can't quench my fire, but I'll play your little game." He glanced right and left. "My personal guard told me Nebuchadnezzar took the mercenaries as well as his Babylonian troops. I suspect the Egyptians have honored our treaty and drawn him away, but I'll find out more at the council meeting." Tracing his finger along my jawline, his eyes raked me with ungranted familiarity. Withdrawing a coin from his waist pouch, he tossed it into the basket at my feet. "I'll give you more information and three more pieces of silver if you come home with me after the meeting."

I ducked my head, feigning shyness to hide my revulsion. "You flatter me with your attention, Lord Jehukal." I nodded at my harps on display. "If you purchased one of my harps, I could spend less time in the market tomorrow and offer your wife lessons—so she might please you with the same songs I play."

His bawdy laughter drew the attention of the growing crowd. "If I wanted a harp, Merari, I would buy one from the Babylonian merchants. Your harps are pretty little baubles, but when Nebuchadnezzar took our best soldiers and artisans, I stopped buying anything in Jerusalem." He walked away laughing, and my cheeks burned at the smirks from onlookers.

Furious, I began wrapping my *pretty little baubles* in thick blankets and placing them in my small wagon. That fat nobleman had no idea what craft and skill were involved in carving, drying, and stringing a harp. He was an imbecile. A fool.

Like our King Zedekiah. Did he really think Egypt could save Judah from King Nebuchadnezzar's minions? When the siege began, market gossips talked of six nations fighting with the Babylonians. Edomites, of course. They found any excuse to harass us, still bitter generations after Jacob cheated Esau out of his birthright. Arabs, Persians, Scythians, Medes, and Syrians also joined the threat, all anxious to curry the favor of Nebuchadnezzar, the man who had conquered the invincible Assyrians. But Babylon's king possessed something far greater than mercenary armies and more valuable than his military mind. According to Yahweh and His prophet Jeremiah, Nebuchadnezzar was God's designated instrument of wrath on Judah. He held God's favor, which meant he could not fail.

I placed my last harp in the wagon and a commotion near the Temple gate drew my attention. Jeremiah. A temple guard dragged him by the neck toward the palace.

"Stop!" I ran toward them, leaving my wagon. "Stop! What are you doing? He's done nothing but speak truth."

I realized the guard was Irijah, brother of Jehukal. "He was deserting to the Babylonians." He pulled Jeremiah backward such that he couldn't get his footing.

"No," Jeremiah croaked, scratching at the arm cutting off his airway. "I wasn't."

"At least let him stand." I tugged at Irijah's arm, trying to loosen his grip. "You're choking him!"

The guard shoved me aside. "The council can decide, but I know what I saw. He deserves death."

A shiver worked up my spine as he dragged my cousin up the palace steps. Would Irijah finally have his vengeance? Five years ago, a priest on the king's council falsely prophesied that Yahweh would deliver Judah and its king from Babylon's yoke of oppression. The priest's name was Hananiah—Irijah and Jehukal's *abba*. Jeremiah issued Yahweh's judgment on Hananiah for his false prophecy, and within two months he was dead. His sons never forgave Jeremiah, and today they would no doubt seek to repay him.

CHAPTER 2

"Jeremiah was put into a vaulted cell in a dungeon, where he
remained a long time.
Then King Zedekiah sent for him and had him brought to the palace,
where he asked him privately, 'Is there any word from the LORD?'
'Yes,' Jeremiah replied, 'you will be delivered into the hands of the
king of Babylon.'"
-Jeremiah 37:16–17

I wanted to follow Irijah but remembered my wagon
full of harps. Hustling back to my booth, I found
the wagon where I left it, untouched. Even Jerusalem's thieves
must be distracted by Jeremiah's arrest. Angry and helpless, I
began my torturous walk home, traveling against the flow of
curious citizens. Though the cobblestone streets of the upper
city hadn't changed, and the dividing archway between upper
and lower city towered over me—today's downhill journey
into Jerusalem's poorest sectors felt like passing from Paradise
to Sheol.

During the two weeks of siege in the upper city, citizens

experienced little more than inconvenience. Their grain and food supplies had been stockpiled for months, and King Hezekiah's ancient tunnel continued to channel water inside our city walls. My wagon wheels splashed into the trench flowing through the lower city's main street, splashing waste—both human and animal—on my robe. Everything from the upper city flowed downhill, except the prosperity. Except the food.

During the two-week siege, we in the lower city had already become desperate for food. My neighbors sold a few furniture pieces to pay for grain, and I offered to a vendor in the upper city two of Jehukal's silver coins for a handful of barley. Outrageous, but what else could we do?

When the Babylonians attacked Jerusalem nine years ago, we hadn't endured a siege. King Jehoiachin simply opened the gates and let them in, allowing Nebuchadnezzar to take our best soldiers and artisans. Which was wiser? My stomach growled. According to Jeremiah, if Zedekiah refused to surrender, our minds wouldn't be able to even fathom the horror we'd experience within these walls during the siege to come.

Veering down a narrow alley north of my house, I knocked on a rickety door and called inside. "Ruth? Abigail? Are you home?"

"Merari? Is that your sweet voice?"

I nudged the door open, and Ruth met me there. She was the spryest of the two widows. I waved Abigail back to her cushion. "Don't get up. I can't stay long." These women had become like second imas to me when Yahweh's faithful in Jerusalem began meeting with Jeremiah after the exile nine years ago.

"Why the trumpets?" Ruth asked. "We heard the trumpets

and felt the ground shake. Did the Babylonians leave? Have you talked to Jeremiah?"

I released a shuddering breath. "The Babylonians are gone, but we don't know why or for how long. Remember what Jeremiah said though. Babylon will eventually destroy Jerusalem and kill the king, his family, and his officials if he doesn't surrender."

This brought Abigail to her feet with great effort. "So Nebuchadnezzar's army will come back?"

The fear in her eyes made me ache to reassure her, but how could I? "Yes, they'll be back. And . . ."

Exchanging a glance, they asked in unison, "What?"

"One of Hananiah's sons arrested Jeremiah as a traitor." Their wrinkled hands covered fearful gasps. "I must get home to Taphath and Neriah, but I'll stop by Caleb's house first and ask him to notify the others in our fellowship. Perhaps he could run back to the upper city and wait for a public verdict to be announced."

"I'll tell Caleb." Ruth had already grabbed her head scarf and cloak and was moving toward the door. "You go home."

I blew Abigail a kiss, hugged Ruth, and then hurried out the door, sending a quick prayer heavenward. *Yahweh, protect Your servant Jeremiah, and protect me now as I return home to my sister. Give me grace to love her well and wisdom to draw her back to You.*

The sun had disappeared behind the western hills, so I walked home in the dim, gray hues of dusk. My wagon rattled behind me on the pitted, filthy streets of the lower city's squalor. I shivered. Was it the biting cold, or the awful memory of Irijah's arm cinched tight around Jeremiah's neck?

I shook my head and determined to focus on the joy in my life. Neriah, my son. He was my reason for breathing. He was why I endured leering hyenas like Jehukal.

I rounded the last corner in the southernmost section of town and found a lamp burning in our single window. A sign Taphath was having a good day. Perhaps we could enjoy a nice meal before bedtime.

When was the last time I'd enjoyed anything with my sister? It had been nine years since the Babylonians stole Elon and our parents and the children. And killed Taphath's betrothed. He resisted capture, and the Babylonians attacked him like a mosquito on a summer day. They left his body in the Kidron Valley to be picked apart by scavengers. Taphath disappeared for days after, and I thought I'd lost her too. She returned to me wearing the image of a bull's head around her neck, and I realized I had indeed lost her—to Molech, an enemy deadlier than Babylon.

"*Ima*, you're home!" Neriah hugged my waist. "We heard the Babylonians leave! *Doda* Taphath said we could go outside the city tomorrow and search their campsite."

"You're not leaving the city, Neriah." I cast a burning gaze at my sister, who sat beside the cook fire, sipping porridge as thin as the widows'. "The armies have gone, but they're coming back. Jeremiah said they'll destroy Jerusalem. We're staying inside these walls."

Taphath rolled her eyes. "Jeremiah is an old coot who likes to scare little boys and old women." She sneered at Neriah. "Stop hanging on your ima like that. You're not a baby anymore."

I squeezed him tighter and kissed the top of his head. "You're never too old to be loved." Neriah buried his face against me, a rambunctious boy in need of reassurance after tonight's frightening events. My eyes burned into my sister. "Must you always speak harshly?"

"Will you hide him in your skirts until the Babylonians find him there?"

Fury like a desert wind rose inside me, and I nudged my boy aside. "Get out, Taphath. You've done enough damage tonight. Go . . . wherever it is you go."

She looked up with a snide grin and set aside her bowl. "You mean I'm dismissed, now that the royal princess has returned?"

There it was. The perpetual accusation. "You think my life is easier than yours, Taphath?"

Neriah retreated to a corner, listening to the discordant strains of our recurring chorus. "If you would focus on Yahweh's blessings rather than your loss . . ."

"I look to Molech for my provision now, Sister." She lifted the horned-ox pendant at her neck and shook it at me. "At least he gives me pleasure with the pain." She stormed out the door, slamming it behind her.

"Why does she worship Molech when she knows it's wrong, Ima?" Neriah's voice was barely over a whisper, my ten-year-old asking the question the prophets had been shouting for generations.

"Never mind. Let's eat."

While I dipped his portion into a bowl, he laid his arm over my shoulder. "It's all right, Ima. She'll be back tomorrow, and I'll talk with her. She's not as angry when it's only her and me." He kissed my cheek and took the bowl, beginning the Shema before we ate our meal. "Hear, O Israel: The LORD our God, the LORD is one. Love the LORD your God with all your heart and with all your soul and with all your strength . . ."

With a weary sigh, and feeling like a complete failure, I joined him in prayer. ". . . we will fear the LORD our God, serve Him only and take our oaths in Your name. Let it always be so in the lives of Your people." I drew him into my arms and whispered, "And may it someday be so in Taphath's life again."

Jeremiah's arrest flashed across my memory, and I squeezed my eyes tight, dreading this moment. Neriah adored the old prophet, and Jeremiah—never having a wife or children—doted on my boy like his own grandson.

I wiped both our tears with my head scarf and braced his shoulders for the news. "They've taken Jeremiah before the king's council as a traitor."

He jumped to his feet, tears welling up, while thoughts rushed behind those large, dark eyes. "What will they do to him?"

I stood and pulled him into a gentle hug. "We must pray they do nothing until Nebuchadnezzar returns with his armies and proves Jeremiah's prophecies correct. Then, they won't dare harm Yahweh's anointed."

CHAPTER 3

IDAN, JERUSALEM - TWO YEARS LATER

*"For this is what the L*ORD *says about the sons and daughters born in [Jerusalem] . . . :*
'They will die of deadly diseases.
They will not be mourned or buried but will be like dung lying on the ground.
They will perish by sword and famine,
and their dead bodies will become food for the birds and the wild animals.'"
-Jeremiah 16:3–4

*W*ith a final heave, my men and I shoved the mammoth log forward on its wheels and heard Jerusalem's Horse Gate crack open like an egg. A valiant cheer, and every one of us rushed in with battle axes held high, hearts pumping battle fury into our veins. More soldiers joined my brother Scythians and me—Medes, Syrians, Edomites—many nations who fought with Nebuchadnezzar's army by choice or conscription.

We rushed into the streets, surging into what must have

once been their market. We'd barely gone a stone's throw, when our victory cries died and we gawked like maidens. A pile of bones lay in the street—human bones—stacked as high as a man. Some were charred as if burned in a fire. Some still bore flesh. Why hadn't they surrendered? A people should know when they've been conquered. Revulsion stirred the fury in my blood.

A few Medes retched beside me. "Go home to your mothers!" I laughed as did my men. A Scythian was born for war. "Follow me, Scythians! We clear the southern city. Kill the weak. Capture those who can survive the march to Babylon." The fetid stench of death and disease prophesied few captives in the train.

I led one hundred of my best Scythian warriors through a large archway that apparently divided the wealthier part of the city from squalor. These were under my direct command, their bows and battle axes clanging in perfect rhythm against their backs. Three thousand more fought alongside Nebuchadnezzar's disciplined troops. He was King of the World, a man worth fighting for—so said my father Saulius, king of the Scythians.

The familiar bitterness reignited my rage, and I released another roar. Survivors scurried at the sound of our approach, out of the streets and into their homes. Did they think they could hide? One man crawled across the threshold of his mudbrick hovel. I sent him to the land of dead Jews with a single swipe of my axe. Where did their god take them—a god who would allow this kind of degradation to visit his people?

My orders were simple in the southern city, but General Nebuzaradan's were more complex in the northern district. He must search among the survivors for a holy man called *Jeremiah*. Nebuchadnezzar sought to reward him with kinder treatment. Why was the King of the World so fascinated by the Jews' god and his prophet? He'd even given strict orders about dismantling the golden temple. Frustration mounted, and I released it through my battle axe. Three less captives to feed and chain.

Death cries echoed behind me as my men did their work. I paused a moment in the street, eyes guzzling the depravity and watering at the stench. How many of these survivors could actually survive the march? The best of them looked like skeletons with skin stretched over bones. Could any endure a forty-day journey to Babylon?

Nebuchadnezzar warned me and the other commanders when the siege began eighteen months ago, "These Judeans are like iron. Once they're bent in a direction, they're impossible to straighten." His chief wise man had been taken from Jerusalem as a boy, and even he called his people *stiff-necked*.

"And now your neck is broken, stubborn mule." I spoke to a man half-conscious as my axe sped his journey to the land of the dead.

Jerusalem's southern-most wall towered before me, and I heard Nebuchadnezzar's troops battering through the other side. They'd breach it soon enough, destroying the dwellings within the wall as well as the people—or bodies—inside. I'd seen more dead than alive on my journey and counted no more than fifty on the main street who might endure the march. Having reached the gate, I turned to assess our work so far. My chest swelled with pride, seeing every one of my warrior's axes dripping with blood. They'd met every challenge I'd asked of them since my father sent us to "defend Scythia's honor" and fight for the King of the World.

Nebuchadnezzar cared nothing about my father or Scythia's honor, but his father, Nabopolassar, held a grudge against Scythia for aligning with Assyria thirty years ago. My men and I paid a high price for a political error made two generations before us, but considering it was my royal family that put us under Babylon's thumb . . .

Finished with my general sweep, it was time to begin the odious work of clearing the filthy hovels. The first stone house I approached smelled of death. Flattening myself against the outer wall beside the door, I pulled out a long strip of cloth from my belt and covered my nose and mouth, knotting it at the back of my leather helmet. I heard flies swarming within, a strong indicator of no survivors, but I'd learned not to take chances.

I leaned into the doorway. "You have one chance to surrender." No response. Not a flutter or whisper.

Distracted by laughter, I looked up the street to find two of my men comparing trinkets. One of them held a silver statue the size of his hand. Idols found in raids had become a contest. Whoever returned to camp with the largest bauble got double portions of food and wine. The thought propelled me into the little house.

While my eyes adjusted to the darkness, I held my battle axe in my right hand, letting it fall to my right, rolling my wrist in a circle—then to my left side in a circle. It was a warrior's mindless habit with a weapon as familiar as my own hands. And then the mundane became unimaginable.

I dropped the axe and rushed outside, bracing myself against the doorframe as I retched. *Great goddess Tabiti, how could a woman do this?* I'd killed thousands, tortured hundreds. Never had I seen the savagery . . .

"What did you find, Commander?" my best friend shouted from across the street.

I stood quickly, kicking dust over my pool of weakness. "I

found gods the size of my toe. You'll surely win my portion of wine tonight, Azat."

He held up a hand-sized idol, victorious, while I gathered my courage to retrieve my battle axe from inside. With a sustaining breath, I turned and waded into the darkness like it was a winter stream.

Keeping my eyes off the carnage, I noted the sparse surroundings. No baskets, dishes, or furnishings. Everything had surely been used to fuel fires during the winter months. A single blanket lay piled in the far corner. Odd. Why wouldn't they have burned it as well?

Remaining focused on the blanket, I stepped around the shadowed horror in my periphery, swatting flies, and swallowing back my morbid curiosity at what had happened here. I leaned over to pick up the mysterious blanket and realized there was something wrapped within it. Squeezing my eyes shut, I sniffed back the unfamiliar sense of hesitation. When had I become a mewling puppy?

I threw my head back and let out another war cry and heard a dozen or more of my men answer their ferocious encouragement. War was my life, my soul, my destiny. Mercenary. Marauder. Scythian. I drew my dagger, snatched the blanket away, and felt my jaw drop. A magnificent harp lay amid the famine, plague, and squalor.

"Oooooh."

I jumped and turned, dagger at the ready, at a woman's low moan. Forcing a deeper search of the dimly lit room, the sound drew me toward the central fire ring. Three bodies lay in the eerie glow of waning sunlight in varying degrees of violence. Only one could have made a sound.

Eyes fluttering, hair matted, the wraith stared at nothing. Heat radiated from her body. I nudged her like a child inspecting eggs in a nest. No response. Had the illness driven her mad, causing her to butcher the other two in her household? I inspected their wounds more closely. *No. No, it can't be.* The boy had been lovingly tended after his death. Something in my gut said this woman had somehow tried to protect him.

"Ta . . ." She breathed out the softest whisper, so I leaned close, and she spoke again. "Ta . . . pe . . ."

I removed the cloth from my head and wetted it with the water from my pouch. Placing it against her cracked lips and pushing it against her swollen tongue, I let the moisture give life. And waited.

Still staring at the wall with her eyes half-closed, she reached for something unseen. "Ta . . . pe . . ."

And suddenly I knew. *Tabiti.* She was saying *Tabiti.* It was the mother goddess of my people, come down in human form! Wonder filled me. Goddess of marriage and home, purity and fidelity. The image of my wife's beautiful face flashed in my mind and then our son. Chest tightening as if in a vice, I could barely breath, so strong was my longing for them. *Tabiti, give me courage to complete these final months of service to Babylon.*

Another low moan startled me from the prayer, and I reached out to touch her cheek. Burning with fever, yes, but now I studied her surroundings with fresh eyes. Carnage, indeed, but only the divine Tabiti could have arranged this scene as a testimony. The boy's broken body lay between us. She had fought for him, fought the woman across the room to protect—or at least venerate—this household. Tabiti, a warrior for her family like me. I glanced at the blanket-wrapped harp in the corner and back at my goddess. It was I who would win the double portions of food and wine tonight. The life-sized goddess was now under my care and protection.

CHAPTER 4

*"The Babylonians broke up the bronze pillars, the movable stands
and the bronze Sea
that were at the temple of the Lord and they . . . also took away the
pots, shovels,
wick trimmers, dishes and all the bronze articles used in the temple
service.
The commander of the imperial guard took away the censers and
sprinkling bowls—
all that were made of pure gold or silver."*
-2 Kings 25:13–15

*A*fter hiding Tabiti and the exquisite harp in my tent
outside the city, I returned to my regiment, continuing to plunder and gather treasure in the southern city. We
worked quickly, finding few people alive and even fewer valuables in the hovels they used for shelter. Poverty had plundered them long before Babylon broke through the gates.

"Commander, over here!" Azat shouted from the north.
"The other troops are destroying the Temple."

I shouted a curse and ran, the few pieces of gold and silver I'd collected jingling in my shoulder bag. Nebuchadnezzar had clearly commanded the Temple to be dismantled last. With care and precision. Where was General Nebuzaradan to control his commanders? And why weren't the other commanders taking charge of their regiments?

My men fell in step at full sprint, proceeding behind me through the archway and into the upper city. The scene was utter chaos. I raised my fist, signaling my men to stop. Searching the mob for Babylon's general, I saw nothing but crazed soldiers, eyes glazed with battle fury. Jerusalem's famed temple was crumbling. No one could stop it now.

Azat, at my right shoulder, raised his voice. "What is your command?"

I shouted at my men, "We are Scythians, unbound by temples or homes of wood and stone. Our wealth is here." I beat my chest with my fist. "The heart of Scythia is our brotherhood. Return to camp, where we'll count our treasures, exaggerate our success, and drink too much wine!"

"Ooh, yah!" My men began their disciplined jog behind me. Azat, as my captain, provided rear guard. Three steps and a shout, "Ooh," battle axe popping forward and back. It was our way. Our intimidation. Enemies trembled at the rhythmic sound of Scythia's approach.

We reached camp in the eastern valley of Kidron. "Dismissed!" I shouted, and the men scattered to their tents. Azat's swagger told me he'd found good treasure. He was no taller than most women—his head barely reaching my armpit—but he was solid muscle and the most ferocious warrior in my regiment.

The mighty little man reached into his shoulder bag, but I

preempted his reveal. "Wait. I have to show you something first." I waved him toward my tent.

He laughed and followed two steps behind. "What are we, ten? You think your prize is better than—"

I opened my tent flap. "She's a gift from the gods, Azat. She's going to lead us home."

His mouth hung open for a moment before his tirade began. "Did a temple pillar fall on your head? She's a *Judean* skeleton with a belly bloated like a pregnant dog." He knelt beside her and rested his ear against her chest. "She's barely breathing."

"I know it's hard to believe, but if you'd been there . . . If you'd seen what she did to the boy in her house, you'd know she is Tabiti."

"Tabiti? Why would our goddess come as a Judean?" He looked around, clasped my shoulder, and lowered his voice. "My friend, this woman has the same plague that killed hundreds in Jerusalem. Our orders were to kill those too weak to travel." He removed his hand from my shoulder and drew his dagger, taking a step toward my goddess.

"No!" I gripped his wrist. "I don't know why Tabiti came as a Judean, but you won't touch her."

"Will you?" His insinuation was an insult.

I answered through gritted teeth. "Tabiti is the goddess of hearth and wealth. She rewards purity and fidelity—"

"I know to whom we pray, Idan. Answer my question. What happens when—if—this woman recovers?" Azat held open the tent flap and examined her more closely. "She could be beautiful if not burning with fever and writhing with chills." He dropped the flap. "Can you remain faithful to Zoya with Tabiti in your tent?"

I lifted my chin. "Tabiti will help me remain faithful to Zoya."

Azat squeezed the back of his neck. "I'm not going to talk you out of this, am I?"

"She is Tabiti, Azat. I'm sure of it."

He sighed. "All right, but we wait to tell the men until they've had plenty of wine tonight. They obey us without question, but some of the unmarried ones will struggle to leave a woman untouched—goddess or not."

Since we were the first regiment to return from plunder, I sent out six hunting parties to help provide the camp's evening meal. Four returned with multiple deer, and I exchanged a triumphant glance with Azat. Tabiti's blessings had already begun.

While we watched sizzling, juicy venison turn on the spits, Babylon's raiding parties trickled back to their camps, heavy laden with gold, bronze, and silver. Many pulled oversized carts like oxen because the bounty was more than they could carry.

I pointed a meaty finger at the imbeciles. "How do you suppose they'll get all that home?" My men laughed loud and long, having fought for many nations as paid warriors. The bounty always went to the king—no matter who scavenged it. Every piece of bronze, gold, and silver from Jerusalem's temple would land in Babylon's treasuries. My warriors, on the other hand, would reveal our treasures to each other by the fire and then hide them in our bags and blankets. Babylon couldn't take what it didn't know we had.

"It's time to compare today's bounty, boys," I shouted at my hundred-man regiment. The other three thousand Scythians were under the command of my captains, also in regiments of hundreds, enjoying the same camaraderie around the fires surrounding us tonight. "Who will get double portions of food and wine?" Any competition stirred their blood to boiling.

Women we'd acquired along the way kept our wine cups full as each warrior held the wood, stone, or metal idols aloft. Some treasures received whistles and cheers. A few were ridiculed. I waited to reveal my find until last.

"Are there any more? I don't want to miss anyone." My men exchanged suspicious glances, knowing I was never so gracious as when I was certain of victory. "I've hidden mine in my tent. Azat, would you help me retrieve it?"

He rolled his eyes, no doubt thinking my antics unnecessary, but I loved a well-fought win. I lifted the limp goddess into my arms and returned the five paces to our fire. Silence met me, expressions sober regardless of the wine.

"Even as you, my fiercest warriors, have committed your swords to fight and someday secure for me Scythia's throne, today the gods have shown their favor as well." I lifted the wraith-like form toward the heavens and shouted, "Mother goddess, Tabiti, from this moment forward, we vow our allegiance, our protection, and our honor to you. Give us success on this our final campaign for Babylon, and lead us safely home to our families."

An awkward silence made my skin crawl, and for less than a heartbeat, I feared rebellion. But the mighty little man beside me raised his war cry. Every soldier leapt to his feet and joined him. The brotherhood of Scythia spread to all our regiments. Swords in hands. Scythia in hearts. The goddess in my arms.

CHAPTER 5

MERARI

"See, I am doing a new thing! Now it springs up; do you not perceive it?
I am making a way in the wilderness and streams in the wasteland."
-Isaiah 43:19

I fluttered on the edge of consciousness, unable to wake but unwilling to dream. What strange sound invaded my stupor? A *boinging, boing, boing* in rhythm with my body's bouncing and the pounding of my head. Dimness swallowed the light, and once again I was taken away . . .

My eyelids felt like gates of iron, and darkness pressed against my body like a heavy blanket. I was lying flat on the ground, no longer jolted as a burden on a beast's back. Heavy breathing beside me sounded like a growl. Was it real or had a creature of Sheol come to claim me for my sins? I tried to scream, to open my eyes, but I was chained inside the prison of my mind. My head pounded; body ached; I coughed. The effort drained me, and blinding fog claimed me again . . .

Cool water touched my face, my arms, my legs and feet.

Soothing. Cleansing. Like stepping into the waters of the *mikveh* after my monthly flow. I let the dream carry me into delight. No more fear of creatures in the darkness, only a soft glow and warmth all around me. Distant laughter and men's voices invaded, and I began to fight the hands that held me. I tried to open my eyes. My arms and legs felt like weights. A gentle voice whispered, *"Shh,"* and strong arms lifted me, cradled me, drew me close. I faded peacefully into the warm glow . . .

Aware of a now-familiar sound on the edges of my consciousness—*boing, boing, boing*—my eyelids barely opened. Darkness filled a tent half my height and was lit by a sliver of moonlight shining through a slit in dark canvas. I was alone, surrounded by sparse furnishings. Two cups. Two bowls. A bow and a quiver full of arrows.

I lifted my hand into the single ray of moonlight. Yes, it was real. I was awake. I pressed my hand to my face and winced at the heat. My head still throbbed, but at least I moved.

At the sound of men's bawdy laughter outside the tent, I covered a sob and pressed down panic. Who were they, and how did I get in a tent? Whose weapons lay beside me? A battle axe. A bow and quiver of arrows. The awful *boinging* sound continued, now accompanied by men's singing in a language I'd never heard. Laughing and shouting mingled. I covered my head and used all my strength to turn on my side, away from the tent opening. Away from my source of terror.

Arms over my ears dulled the noise, but not the memories. "Neriah." Whispering my son's name gouged my soul with deep wounds. Sobs shook me, draining what little strength I had.

"Tabiti wakes." A man's broken Hebrew replaced grief with

panic. Too weak to fight, my pathetic attempt to scoot away was blocked by the tent wall.

"*Shh.*" A huge hand stroked my hair.

Recognition filled me with horror. "You washed me!" I screeched in Aramaic. Like a limp fish, I fell onto my back and gazed into almond-shaped eyes.

A small lamp lit the tent, revealing a pleased expression on a creature from another world. "Of course, Tabiti would know the language of trade. It's how we speak to the Babylonians as well." Terrifying tattoos covered every part of his neck, arms, legs, and chest. An angry scar bisected the right side of his face from the nose to his ear, and heavy, black brows peaked in the middle as if he was constantly questioning. I could only whimper and shake at the sight of him.

"You need not fear, Tabiti. No one will harm you." He reached out to touch my face, and I released a piteous howl. "*Shh. Sleep now.*" He held a wooden cup of liquid to my lips, and I drank, still shivering. Was it fever's chill or terror?

After three more sips of bitter liquid, he left the tent. I lifted the lightweight blanket covering me and found myself dressed in a new red robe—red, the color of harlotry. What had they done to my body while I lay unaware? My cheeks burned, and indignation drained my strength. A distant roar mingled with gray splotches, and I realized it must have been something in the drink. Before I could think what it might have been, darkness claimed me again.

A rough hand patted my cheek, rude and persistent. The hulking creature crouched before me, speaking, but I couldn't hear him. Without permission, he laid down beside me, curving his mountainous frame around mine. I wanted to push him away, to kick and scream, but my body was limp. A helpless slab of meat in a butcher's hands.

But he didn't hurt me. Why? Instead, he held me gently, as if I might break, and his hands didn't wander or violate. *Yahweh, help me!* The barbarian hummed softly, stealing my consciousness with his soothing presence.

"Tabiti." I heard a whisper in my sleep. A gentle breath on my cheek stirred my senses. "Tabiti, dawn comes."

Like a crashing cymbal, the words jarred me awake with the memory of last night's intruder. His arms and legs wrapped me like a cocoon in an intimacy I'd known only with beloved Elon. My heart rent at the thought of what this stranger might have done to me, and I released a sound that could have curdled milk. The barbarian scuttled to his feet as if I'd bitten him. Perhaps I'd do exactly that if he came near me again.

"What? What is it?" He stood over me, short-cropped black hair hugging his startled face. "Are you hurt?"

Again, he spoke in Hebrew. I refused to answer. When he took a step toward me, I screamed with surprising strength.

"*Shh!* I won't hurt you." The first lines of frustration creased his brow. "I've met your every human need, Tabiti, and I vowed to guard your purity on this journey as I would protect my own wife." Before I could scream again or rail at him with questions, he knelt with his face to the earth and his hands outstretched—as if I were royalty.

Confusion gave rise to panic. Surely, I was having a nightmare or dying from the plague in Jerusalem like so many others. I was delirious, imagining the barbarian. Beside me sat a polished bronze mirror. I reached for it. I don't know why, but when I saw my reflection, I knew—this was no dream. I saw my sister's face staring back at me. Lifeless. Haunted. As she'd been the morning she killed my son.

"Do you like the mirror, Tabiti?" The man sat back on his

heels. "I bought it for you yesterday, when we passed through Megiddo."

"Megiddo? That's three days north of Jerusalem."

"We left Jerusalem the day after I found you." He reached out to touch my hair, but I swatted it away. His frustration returned. "Leaving was your only hope of protection, Tabiti. The general lost control of his troops. My men will respect you, but I couldn't protect you against the other nations who care nothing about the Scythian goddess of—"

"Did I hear the shriek of a goddess?" Another man, much shorter than the giant, poked his head through the tent flap. I gasped, but he ignored me. "We should go if we're to reach Hazor by nightfall."

"We'll be ready, Azat." The barbarian searched my gaze as he spoke. "She's a bit disoriented. She doesn't seem to realize she's Tabiti."

"*Hmm.*" The non-committal grunt punctuated the second man's departure.

I turned away, too tired to care about the consequences. "Why do you protect me, and who is *Tabiti?*"

He ignored my questions and packed the tent's sparse contents into his shoulder bag. Lying helpless, too strong to faint and too weak to move, I wished for unconsciousness. The barbarian lifted the tent off the ground, leaving me exposed to the already oppressive summer heat. Rolling the tent into a bundle, he secured it with other supplies on a donkey and then scooped me off my reed mat, held me in one arm, and in one fluid motion landed both of us on a sleek, black stallion. Repositioning me in his arm like a nursing babe, I could do nothing but cover my face in shame.

Someone attached something behind my captor's saddle—my reed mat, I presumed. "Thank you, Azat." While cradling me in his right arm, he waved his left arm forward, releasing an ear-splitting whistle. The horse beneath us reared slightly and shot into a gallop like a stone from a sling, while the sound of thundering hooves exploded behind us.

I groaned at the pounding, lifting my hand to steady my head against his chest. He shoved my hand away and repositioned me again, holding my head to his chest for me—and then my eyes went wide with panic. "How are you holding the reins?" Fighting his grasp to look at his position, I felt his first show of force.

He held me tighter and grinned, one arm cradling me, the other hand on my cheek. "I rode a horse before I could walk. You are safe, Tabiti."

Without permission, my body melted into his strength. The excitement had drained me, and I didn't even care where we were going.

He curled his arms up, drawing me close. "You have defeated death, Tabiti. Rejoice. I will present you to Nebuchadnezzar in Riblah and then take you home. Finally, home."

Home. I let my heavy eyelids close, aching at the thought of starting over in Babylon. Could I live without Neriah? Would my grief ever end? My eyes shot open with a ray of new hope. *Yahweh, could You lead me to Elon in Babylon?*

CHAPTER 6

IDAN, HAZOR

"Hazor will become a haunt of jackals, a desolate place forever.
No one will live there; no people will dwell in it."
-Jeremiah 49:33

The goddess slept in my arms while traveling through the tropical terrain bordering Lake Kinneret and following the Jordan River north. Peace softened her features now, but the turmoil I'd glimpsed in her liquid brown eyes this morning was seared into my memory. How could divine Tabiti not realize she'd poured herself into human form? Had the under-gods Papaeus and Api confused her mind? Had I somehow stepped into a civil war among Scythia's gods?

Troubled by what-ifs, I couldn't look away from her. Even the dark circles of famine-gaunt cheekbones were striking on the divine-made-flesh.

"If you want to speak with her, jostle her awake." Azat rode up beside me, wearing the impish grin of a lifelong friend. He looked over his shoulder and lowered his voice. "Or have you finally decided she's merely human?"

The question deserved no answer, and I let my angry stare burn him.

Hands lifted in surrender, his smile disappeared. "I'm sorry, but my concern is valid. Our regiment trusts you completely, but we may need more proof for the other commanders and troops."

I dared not disclose my doubts, not even to my best friend. When I found her she'd whispered the goddess' name—hadn't she? "Why must Scythia's crown prince *prove* anything? Haven't I won their allegiance with my axe and blood? This is our last of five campaigns with King Nebuchadnezzar. Have they forgotten that Babylon's favor will give me the influence I need to challenge my father's throne?"

"We haven't forgotten, my friend." Azat slammed his fist over his heart and kept his voice low. "You are already our king, but we must continue to cultivate the men's loyalty. Your father forgot this, and it has already cost him his son. It will soon cost him his throne."

He was right. "What can I do to convince them she is Tabiti?"

Azat remained silent for a time, riding beside me in comfortable silence. I wondered if he'd forgotten my question until a deep sigh told me he'd finished contemplating. "Our warriors must believe the heavens will rain down fire if they defile this woman who represents Tabiti's fidelity and purity. Most of those who have wives, as you do, have remained faithful on this long campaign with Nebuchadnezzar, but when they saw you sharing your tent with her—"

"I would not defile the goddess!" The declaration was more adamant than I intended.

My friend's brows rose. "Your determination is strong, but no man is made of iron. If you keep holding her as you are now . . ."

I looked down at her. The vulnerability alone stirred my blood. Azat was wise, and he knew me too well. I focused on the path before us and my wife's face flashed in my mind. I tried to summon an image of our infant son but couldn't. I saw only Zoya holding the small bundle in her arms, tears streaking her lovely face as I rode away. It had been a year since I'd left, but it felt like a decade.

Arms burning from four days of bearing the goddess' weight from dawn to dusk, I turned to my friend and finally confessed. "She was unconscious when I found her, but her lips were moving. She whispered what sounded like *Tabiti*. If you had been there, Azat . . ." Was I trying to convince him or myself? "If you had seen how she cared for the boy after death. If you'd seen the feral judgment she meted out against the other woman . . ."

"Then tell me. Tell me so I can—"

"No!" I stared at him hard. "I vowed to the gods. The scene was sacred."

He nodded, focused on the road ahead. "Our men will defend you unto death, but when we arrive in Riblah, Nebuchadnezzar's men won't care that she's a goddess."

"Then we will make them care." I was finished defending my decision.

Azat dropped his reins and laced his fingers behind his head, releasing a weary sigh. His stallion walked freely as mine had done since this morning. Our fathers had placed us on ponies before we could walk. His life and mine had taken the same path—except his parents had died when he was very young. He was taken into our household, but it was I who would become king and Azat would choose his position on my council. He was more loyal than my brothers and closer to my heart than the flesh on my bones.

As the sun touched the mountaintops at my left, I spotted several lines of smoke ahead and asked Azat, "How many men did you send before us?"

"Ten. Our meal should be ready when we arrive."

And it was. Ten perfect gazelles turned on spits while our weary regiment plodded into a clearing an arrow's flight from the burned-out city of Hazor. Our early arrivers had set fires in a circle, marking an ample area for tonight's camp. I thought it an extravagance until I dismounted with the goddess in my arms. The abandoned city and looming darkness made us a tempting target for an inordinate amount of wildlife.

Tall grass swayed around the perimeter of camp as the last rays of sun reflected on glowing eyes hidden within. Wolves howled, echoing in the distant mountains—a sound I hadn't heard since leaving home. The hair on my neck stood on end.

I laid the goddess on the ground and shouted, "Circle the perimeter, bows drawn!"

"Yes, Commander."

The goddess stirred. "What's happening?"

My stallion pranced sideways, throwing its head left then right. Glowing eyes emerged from the grass, at least a hundred jackals, coming from all sides.

Before I signaled to loose arrows, the woman released a sound unlike any I'd heard. An undulating, throaty call. Both startling and exquisite. Strange and intriguing.

My warriors lowered their bows and stared. All night sounds stilled. And the jackals ceased their advance, perking their ears.

"What are you doing?" My question, asked in wonder, sounded more like censure.

Disdain filled her eyes. She lifted her chin and released the sound again, her tongue tapping her lips to vary the timing and tones.

A strange sight stole my words and chilled my bones. Like a curtain pulled across the evening sky, thousands of birds appeared from the north, blocking the moon and stars. Slack-jawed, I watched the stalking jackals scatter beneath the pressing threat of aerial attack—predators retreating from prey. The birds descended nearby, splashing in the marshes beside Lake Huleh.

I considered the goddess with renewed wonder, all doubts of her deity erased. As a boy, our shaman taught young warriors to be kind to animals because Tabiti protected them, but I'd never seen proof of it—until now.

I prostrated myself before her. "O pure and powerful Tabiti! I vow to you my willing service. Protect the men in my company, and in return receive my devotion as the first of many gifts—" My words lost in the raucous cheering of one hundred Scythian warriors, I lifted my head and found the goddess' face covered with both hands.

I crawled to her and lifted her hands away. She was crying. "What is it? What's wrong?"

"I am not this goddess you seek!" she shouted.

My men didn't hear, and my heart wouldn't believe. Perhaps her denials were a test—a test I would pass. May Tabiti live forever.

CHAPTER 7

MERARI

"Even the stork in the sky knows her appointed seasons, and the dove,
the swift and the thrush observe the time of their migration.
But my people do not know the requirements of the Lord.*"*
-Jeremiah 8:7

*H*ave men no sense? Don't they know birds migrate
in the winter? We simply happened upon an area
where an extraordinary number of birds decided to migrate at
this moment.

Or did You do this, Yahweh? But why would El-Shaddai send
a flock of birds to frighten away jackals, saving a band of
heathens and a worthless woman from Judah? None of it made
sense. In my fear of the stalking jackals, I'd released the loudest
sound my body could produce in its weakened state. I'd used
the ululating only when calling Neriah home. It was a sound
precious to me. A sound I hadn't made since the siege began.
Why did I remember it now? *Yahweh, are You still with me?*

The noise around me was deafening. Warriors clanged
their weapons against shields, some shouting, some laughing.

All of them stood too close, eyes focused on me. I covered my head and pulled my knees to my chest, wishing I could disappear. Was I the only one who knew I wasn't a Scythian goddess?

Idan's presence overshadowed me, and the warmth of his breath tickled my ear. "Azat has set up our tent. Come, lovely Tabiti." Without waiting for my response, he lifted me as if I were a sack of grain.

A cheer rose from the soldiers, and I winced, my head pounding with the noise. "Please, tell them to celebrate quietly."

"It will be as you say, Tabiti." The brightness in his voice spurred a new thought. How far could I press his favor?

Locking his cheeks between my hands, I forced him to meet my gaze. "Tabiti refuses to meet Nebuchadnezzar at Riblah," I blurted. "We will go directly to Babylon. I must find someone there."

He stopped walking and stared at me for three heartbeats. "We must go to Riblah." He ducked into the dark tent before I could argue. "Nebuchadnezzar must see my goddess and know I'm favored above my father. Then he'll award me with gold and troops to take back to Scythia so I can take my father's throne."

"But I must find someone in Babylon." I tried not to sound petulant, but my patience was consumed by my fevered mind.

Idan folded his legs beneath him and cradled me in his lap. Though I couldn't see his face, I sensed increased tension in his arms. Why wasn't he answering me?

"Well? Are we going to Babylon?"

"Babylon is a large country in Nebuchadnezzar's vast empire. Who does Tabiti wish to find there?"

"I . . . I . . ." I couldn't tell him I wanted to find my husband.

"The one you seek could live in Syria, Cilicia, Arabia, or Media. These, too, submit to Nebuchadnezzar's authority. Where should we look first?"

"I don't know," came out in a whisper, and I buried my face against his chest.

He began rocking me, fiddling with something at his waist while I lay like a dead fish in the bend of his arm. I closed my eyes, hoping sleep would claim me, but I heard that awful *boing, boinging* sound and my head shot up.

Holding a small, three-pronged instrument in his mouth with one hand, his abdomen heaved in and out as he played a lively tune. Mesmerized, I forgot to hate him for a moment and admired his talent. It couldn't be easy to change tone and rhythm with breath and tongue on a carved piece of wood.

The distraction worked only for a while. "Tabiti still refuses to meet King Nebuchadnezzar," I said over the music and then closed my eyes.

"Aaagh!" He transferred me to the reed mat and scuttled out of the tent.

Sleep came slowly, amid dark images of lurking jackals and tattooed barbarians dancing to the strange sounds of odd instruments. I jerked awake, finding myself cocooned in Idan's arms.

He breathed against my ear. "You're safe. I'm here."

His words filled me with both peace and dread. "Where are you taking me?" I whispered, desperate for him to say Babylon.

He paused before answering, and I wondered if he was still sleeping. He pointed a thick finger at the slit in the tent flaps. "Sunrise is near. See how the sky is purple, not black."

I looked to the amethyst glow outside and knew better than to press him.

After a few more heartbeats, he added, "Today, we travel to Dan."

I squeezed my eyes closed with a measure of relief. At least Dan was a tribe of Israel and had once been Yahweh's land. Though now in the northern reaches of Canaan, I would still celebrate this day. It would be the last time I breathed the air, touched the soil, and drank the water in the land Yahweh promised to Abraham.

Helpless to change my fate, I watched the sky turn from amethyst to red to pink, while a Scythian's heavy breaths warmed my cheek and his arms held me. Even a goddess was captive to the will of men.

CHAPTER 8

*"Charm can be misleading, and beauty is vain and so quickly fades,
but this virtuous woman lives in the wonder, awe, and fear of
the Lord.
She will be praised throughout eternity."*
-Proverbs 31:30

*B*y the time we stopped to refresh at midday, I wanted to die. My body screamed in pain, my head pounded, and my heart felt like an iron ball in my chest.

"Drink." Idan held out a cup of water from a roadside spring. He had propped me against a rock. I had just enough strength to turn away.

"You must drink, Tabiti." He moved the cup to my lips, and I turned my head again. "Is this a test of my patience? I will force you to drink if I must."

Tears fought my shackled emotions. I'd been awake since dawn and rode behind my captor, arms wrapped around his middle. But my arms had begun shaking, and I'd nearly fallen to the ground. My weakness was the reason for our stop.

Idan dropped the cup and cradled my face. "Tabiti, I won't force you to drink. Please don't cry."

If I'd known tears would bend him, I'd have cried days ago. "I'm too weak to ride behind you, but I don't want you to hold me like . . ." I felt heat rise in my cheeks and saw his understanding dawn.

He wiped my tears with his thumbs, a horribly tender thing. "Of course. Tabiti is pure and the goddess of fidelity. You sensed my longing for Zoya." His sadness almost made me pity him. "Forgive me. I miss my wife." He lifted the water cup to my lips again.

A wife? This time I drank, letting the coolness of the water slip down my throat. I rested my head against the rock again, trying to imagine his wife. Was she beautiful? No doubt. How would she feel about another woman lying in her husband's arms?

The thought spurred me to consider travel alternatives. Could I ride one of the supply donkeys? My limp arms mocked the idea. How could I ride alone when I'd been rendered helpless from a single morning leaning on my captor?

"We'll buy a camel with a sedan for you in Dan." His comment startled me from my thoughts.

"A camel? You mean, I'll ride alone?"

An impish grin made him less fierce. "I'm certain you won't flee to Babylon without me."

In that moment, I could have liked him. But I could never forgive him. I could never forget what he and Nebuchadnezzar's siege did to my sister and my son.

I commanded my hand to take the cup from him and gulped down the rest of the water. He offered me a piece of cured meat, and I took it. I had to eat. It was my only chance to see Elon again. The Scythian stared at me in silence, and I returned his gaze without flinching—but my heart wavered. Should I insist he see the truth, that I wasn't his precious goddess? He worshiped Tabiti. Would he kill Merari? The blood-stained tunics testified to the Scythians' violent lives, but I'd seen nothing but compassion from them.

"We must go," he said finally.

I nodded, keeping my eyes locked on his. "I'm ready."

He brushed my cheek and grinned. "You are a stubborn one, Tabiti, but I like the human goddess even better than the wooden one." He scooped me up, and I spent the rest of our journey to Dan in his arms, trying to avoid his gaze.

We arrived at the city after dark, greeted by well-lit gates and a festival in the streets. I shouted over the revelry, "Why wasn't Dan burned like Hazor?"

"Its citizens had been oppressed by Assyria for years, so they welcomed Nebuchadnezzar's army."

The captain, Azat, rode up beside Idan from his place at rear guard. Though much shorter than his commander, he was stocky, extremely muscular, and his eyes were fiercer than a lion's. "We've attracted some attention."

Azat nodded at guards on Dan's city's wall, who were now pointing at the Scythian regiment. Idan lifted his shield, as did his men, and the city's guards returned the gesture. I noted Babylon's lion on every defensive weapon. Dan's guardians resumed their watch, satisfied it seemed.

"Tomorrow, you will buy a camel for the goddess." Idan's command was like a clanging symbol on a quiet morning.

Azat stared at him and then glared at me. "If we wait for the market to open, we'll lose valuable—"

"We'll rest tomorrow and set out for Riblah the next day."

The captain's jaw muscle danced, and I could see his frustration growing. Keeping his voice low, he spoke barely loud enough to hear. "The men grow anxious to reach Riblah and receive their payment from Nebuchadnezzar. If you're tired of carrying the goddess, others can help."

"Make sure the camel has a sedan, not just a saddle. Tabiti must have room to lie down for the journey to Riblah."

"We have barely enough gold to buy food." Azat's voice rose in volume and fervor. "What do I use for a camel with a *sedan?*"

Idan's silence increased the tension, but when he removed a gold band from his arm, Azat's features softened. "I'll find another way, Idan."

"No. This will pay for the camel, meals, and lodging in the inn tonight. Make it happen, my friend." Eyes forward, Idan pressed farther into the city's chaos.

Azat glared at me while accepting the gold band. "Will there be anything else, Commander?"

"Yes." Idan finally glanced at his grouchy friend. "Find a woman to ease your foul humor." The man growled curses and reined his horse away, shouting instructions to his men.

I lifted my head from Idan's chest. "Does Azat hate the goddess, or is he jealous that you're talking more to me than to him?"

His grin widened. "Azat always does what's best for me and our men, but he's never had a wife or child whose needs he must consider before his own." Loud shrieks behind us stole my attention, but Idan chuckled. "That would be my men approving the decision to stay at an inn tonight and have a leisurely day tomorrow. Sometimes Azat worries too much."

The chaos of the city swelled around me, causing my grip to tighten around Idan's waist. He pulled me closer, leaning over to kiss my forehead, while holding his shield and reins in front of me. "Don't worry, my goddess. You're safe in my arms.

Tonight we'll shelter under a real roof." The timbre of his voice and the idea of sharing a bed made me feel anything but safe.

The noise around us lessened, and when he reined the stallion to a halt, I lifted my head to see a three-story, stone building towering over us. Lamplight glowed from a few downstairs windows, but most rooms were dark.

We waited on the stallion only a few moments before Azat walked out of the inn and appeared at Idan's side. "I've purchased all the rooms—and a single room for her." He slid his arms under me, lifting me from my protector. "I'll carry her to a room on the third level. You and I can take turns sleeping *outside* her door."

Without waiting for an answer, he walked toward the inn, steps jarring and arms like iron bars beneath me. He looked down, a cold glint in his eyes. "You will break whatever spell you've cast over my friend, or I'll send you to the realm of the dead—goddess or not."

CHAPTER 9

IDAN

*"Judah's sin is engraved with an iron tool, inscribed with a flint point,
on the tablets of their hearts and . . . beside the spreading trees
and on the high hills."*
-Jeremiah 17:1–2

J woke before dawn to the sound of six snoring
soldiers, wishing for the tenth time I'd guarded
Tabiti's door instead of Azat. He had insisted on taking first
watch outside her chamber after I brought her evening meal.
Why? Tabiti made him tense. Angry. Something about her
unnerved him. I suggested he enjoy one of Dan's prostitutes
while I guarded Tabiti's chamber, but his agitation only grew.
My friend could be moodier than a woman.

The incessant snoring rattled my nerves and launched me
from my straw-stuffed mattress, a comfortable privilege I'd
won in last night's wrestling match. I poured my leftover wine
on the loser's snoring form. He woke cursing me.

I threw the rest of the wine in his face. "You can have the
bed now, you old jackal."

Moonlight allowed me to step over the stinking bodies on my way to the door. I opened and closed it quietly behind me, then walked toward a single torch in the narrow corridor. Its flame fluttered with a cool draft coming from a window at the far end.

Azat was not lying on the reed mat beside Tabiti's chamber.

My walk turned into a run as dread snaked up my spine. I burst into the chamber. "Tabiti!"

She was gone. Her bed empty.

Hurried footsteps behind me triggered my reflexes. I whirled, drawing my dagger. Azat stood in the doorway with a basketful of food.

I ran at him, pinning him by the throat to the wall. "Where is she?"

His eyes, as wild as mine, peered over my shoulder. "I was gone for less than ten heartbeats. She can't be far." He lifted the basket on his arm. "I went to the kitchen so she could break her fast."

"Aaahhh!" I released my frustration and my friend. "You search the back. I'll go out the front."

We ran down the back stairway toward the kitchen, and I headed toward the inn's main stairs. I nearly barreled over a frail figure, halfway down the first flight. "By the gods, woman, what are you doing?"

Tabiti fell against the wall and glanced over her shoulder at me. Her face was pale but defiant. "I'm going to see the sunrise. Alone." Pressing herself against the wall to stand again, she nearly tumbled down the stairs.

I lifted her into my arms. "You can't simply leave whenever you please. Shall I have Azat purchase chains so you won't run away?" Marching back up the stairs, I pondered the conse-quences of shackling a goddess.

47

"I wasn't running away." She laid her head against my chest. "Please. I need to see the sunrise one last time in Yahweh's land."

Her words landed like stones in my belly. Why would my goddess care about the Hebrew god or his land?

Azat met me at the top step, fire in his eyes. He'd heard her too. "She's not Tabiti."

Could I have made such a grievous mistake? The consequences were too grave to consider. I took the basket of food from him. "Tabiti is testing my compassion. She's not strong enough to leave the city and see a sunrise. I'm going to—"

"Idan! She's not—"

"Captain!" I stared, waiting for his submission. His back stiffened like a rod, and I calmed myself. "Please, go to the market today and buy a camel with a sedan. We'll return by midday."

He nodded a curt bow and left without a salute or backward glance. Anyone else, I would have punished—especially, for leaving his post—even if it was only for a few moments to gather the morning's meal.

I resumed the descent down the stairs, and Tabiti looked up at me. "I don't need you to carry me."

But I needed to feel her in my arms. "You're too weak."

"I'm not weak." She laid her head against my shoulder, and my heart beat in rhythm for the first time since leaving her last night.

I hurried through the city as the wine-colored eastern sky lightened to the color of grapes on the vine. Discarded clothing and empty wineskins littered the streets from last night's festival. I shouted at the watchmen to open the gate and let us pass. When he refused to open until after dawn, I persuaded him with only a small bribe of my carved leather wristband. Pink rays now glowed beyond the eastern hills as I rushed up the nearest hill to get the best view for my goddess. At the top stood a spreading terebinth, the perfect spot for morning worship. A statue stood at its right and an intricately-carved pole to its left. Incense still glowed in braziers on both sides from last night's offerings.

I propped Tabiti against the sacred tree and fell to my knees. "Lovely Tabiti, goddess of hearth and wealth, hear my petition—"

"Stop it." Her voice was flat, her eyes focused on the glowing horizon.

Had I displeased her? My eyes wandered to the hundreds of vows and prayers carved into the trunk behind her. "To show my devotion, I'll carve your virtues into the Elon tree."

"No!" She gasped as if I'd struck her. "It's called *Elah* in Hebrew, *terebinth*, not *Elon*, which means *oak*. Never say Elon to me again!" She hid her face against her knees, suddenly unconcerned with the glowing orb rising in the east.

Stunned, I couldn't imagine how I'd lost her favor in a single night. Had Azat poisoned her against me? Not knowing what else to do, I removed my dagger from its sheath, ready to carve my vows into the tree.

At the sing of my dagger released from its sheath, Tabiti lifted her head, closed her eyes, and exposed her neck. "Please make the cut deep and quick."

"What?" The moment was absurd. "You are my supreme goddess. The protector of my life, my future. Why would I cut you?"

She opened her eyes, glancing only a moment at me before turning her gaze to the sun. "Idan, there is only one God who spoke all things into existence—the sun, moon, stars, plants, animals, you, and me." She shook her head with a half-smile.

"I'm not your Scythian goddess, Commander. I'm a Hebrew woman named Merari, who was afraid to tell you the truth and bear your wrath."

Her chin quaked, and I felt as if the earth shifted beneath me. This couldn't be true.

Turning her eyes on me again, I saw despair in the hollowed-out caverns. "Use your dagger, Idan. I don't deserve to breathe."

I pulled her to my chest. "You are my treasure, Tabiti. I'll never let you go."

Like a stillborn lamb, she lay in my arms. "Do you know why Nebuchadnezzar sent you to destroy my people?"

"Your people?" My chest constricted. Was this another test? "If you mean the people of Judah, yes, I know why. We destroyed them because King Zedekiah conspired with Pharaoh Hophra against Nebuchadnezzar's authority."

"No, that's not it at all." She wriggled from my arms and sat beside me. Running her hand over the scarred trunk, she inspected the generations-old carvings. "This is proof of my people's apostasy, Idan. My God, Yahweh, is very jealous. He entered into a covenant with one man, Abraham, to make his descendants the source of salvation for all nations. The Israelites are his descendants, and Yahweh is our Shepherd. He even delivered us from bondage in Egypt—"

"I've heard the legends. Everyone knows of the god who brought plagues on the Beautiful Land and killed Pharaoh's firstborn." But the legends couldn't be true—and if they were, why would his people turn away?

"Yahweh's people have squandered His favor, like a lover too well-loved." She ran her fingers over one of the tree's carvings and read, "Oh, great and mighty Baal, we offer you the first fruits of our land because you, O mighty god of the sky, have looked on our land with favor." She dropped her hands to her lap and shook her head. "Nebuchadnezzar's sword is Yahweh's discipline because, though He offered us tremendous loving-kindness, we betrayed Yahweh by worshiping gods of wood and stone. Baal. Chemosh. Asherah. My sister worshiped Molech—and I did nothing to stop her."

The silence stretched long. Why was she making up these stories? "This is a test," I finally said. "You're testing my loyalty, but did I not already prove it by killing Uncle Anacharsis when he returned from Greece, extolling their gods?"

She looked at me like I was a toad. "I know nothing of your uncle or Greece."

Had the gods somehow stolen her memory? "When I found you in Jerusalem, you were barely conscious, but you said your name, '*Tabiti.*'"

"I don't remember the day you found me, and I've never heard of your goddess Tabiti."

"There was a boy lying beside you."

Squeezing her eyes closed, she sent a stream of tears down her cheeks. "My son, Neriah." She winced when she said his name.

"There was a woman also."

"My sister."

"You killed your sister?" The shock in my tone made her cover her face.

"How do you know I killed her?"

"It was obvious by the . . ." How could I say it without offending the goddess? "Your savage protectiveness matched the divine tenderness shown to the boy's remains."

She shook her head, her shoulders shaking. I tried to pull her hands away. "You need not be ashamed, Tabiti. Your strength was obvious when, barely conscious, you could still whisper the first part of your name. *Ta-ba* . . ."

With a little gasp, she dropped her hands and met my gaze. "I said 'Ta-*ba*'?"

"You said '*Tabiti.*'"

"Did I say the whole name?"

I felt my blood run cold and silently begged my memory to fail. Raising my chin, I spoke with confidence I didn't feel. "You said, 'Ta-*bi.*'"

Shaking her head wildly, she said, "No! I was trying to say 'Taphath'! I was trying to say my sister's name, and you heard wrong." Weeping, she crumbled onto the grassy hill.

I scuttled to my feet, stunned. Confused. Disbelieving. Had *Ta-pha* sounded like *Ta-bi* in my yearning for home—for my wife? How could I have been such a fool? Letting out a moan, I looked down at the biggest mistake of my life. If this woman was a filthy Hebrew, how could I salvage the respect of my troops? Dare I confess my mistake? How could I not?

Revulsion at the sight of her rose in my belly, and I left her there, racing down the hill as if a specter chased me. My frenzy caught the attention of a watchman on the tower, so I swallowed my humiliation and slowed my steps, entering the city with false calm. What should I do now? I couldn't face Azat. My thoughts were a jumble. I needed wine. Lots of wine. Maybe then I would gain wisdom to fix the terrible trick the gods had played on me. I headed for the nearest tavern to numb my pain and sharpen my wits—the Scythian way.

CHAPTER 10

MERARI

*"I know that you delight to set your truth deep in my spirit.
So come into the hidden places of my heart and teach me wisdom."*
-Psalm 51:6

I watched Idan go, and a wave of nausea overwhelmed me. Memories flooded like the smell of week-old stew—stronger as each horrific moment led to the next. Why hadn't I tried harder to stop Taphath's idolatry? Jeremiah had warned our fellowship that the siege-induced famine and plague would cause people to do unspeakable things. I believed everything he said, but, of course, it wouldn't happen to my family. Not my son, my sister, or me.

Feeling raw and vulnerable, I ate bread and hard cheese from Idan's basket and prayed the Scythians would forget me. I drank watered wine straight from the skin and prayed Yahweh would strike me dead. I slept in the shade and pleaded in the haze between wakefulness and sleep for someone from Dan to rescue me. Its citizens had once been pure-blooded Israelites, but they'd been exiled to Assyria generations ago. Now mixed-blooded and pagan, they were as foreign to me as the Scythians who held me captive.

Besides, why would anyone save me—a woman who couldn't protect her own child? A woman who killed her own sister.

The day passed too quickly, and I dreaded Idan's return. The sun fell to the west without any sign of my captor, and the same idolatry that destroyed Jerusalem invaded my quiet terebinth.

A bald-headed priest crested the hill and leaned too close. "You're too thin to serve as Asherah's priestess, but we can fatten you up, and you'll bring in a steady income."

I pushed to my feet and stumbled down the hill to escape the sins of my forefathers. Pausing at the road leading into the city, I pondered escape. South to Egypt? North to Tyre? West lay the Great Sea, and east was Babylon. Where could I go that Idan wouldn't find me? That Nebuchadnezzar didn't rule? A new realization struck me like a blow. Idan no longer needed me. It was I who needed him. Leering men passed me as I made my way back to the city on wobbly legs. The Scythians, though warriors and my enemy, were my only chance

Yahweh, I don't deserve to live, but I want to see Elon again. Help me. Please. Though I was still a prisoner to a weakened body, I was no longer the prisoner of a lie. I'd told Idan the truth. He saved Merari, a Hebrew woman, not his goddess Tabiti. Whether he believed me or not, whether he killed me or not, it was his choice now. And my life was in Yahweh's hands.

I wandered in the gray haze of dusk, musicians and dancers celebrating in Dan's streets. By the time I was bumped and jostled through the central thoroughfare, I was disoriented and could barely stand. Festivities grew wilder. Wine and music flowed freely. I turned down side streets, resting often. Panic rose. Truth took root.

I was lost in a foreign city with no money, no help, and little strength left.

Leaning against a stone house, I looked up and down the street, searching for anything familiar. Nothing.

Yahweh, help me! I slid down the stone wall and landed hard on my backside. Vision tunneling black around the edges, I barely clung to consciousness.

"Tabiti!"

The distant shout was like a slap. "Idan!" My voice was lost in the revelry. "Idan," I tried again. My head lolled to the side. "Idan." This time, barely a whisper.

The outline of a figure loomed over me. "Idan?"

"If you're the strongest of Scythia's goddesses, we have no hope." Azat pulled me to my feet and circled my waist, dragging me down the crowded street.

I hoped he was taking me to the inn, but I didn't even care.

I woke choking on warm liquid, poured into my mouth and down my chin. Struggling to sit up, I fought Idan with the cup and Azat holding my shoulders to the bed.

"Drink." Idan kept pouring the foul-tasting potion while I sputtered. He lifted the empty cup away at the same time Azat released me.

I turned on my side and shuddered. "What was that?"

"Acacia tea with coriander and garlic." I could hear the sneer in Azat's voice. "I hope it tasted as bad as it smells."

I shuddered again and gagged, nearly giving it back all over the mattress.

"Don't you dare." Idan pressed my shoulder against the bed and clapped his hand over my mouth. "The priest said you will drink it four times a day to regain your strength. We've made enough to last four days' travel to Riblah."

I nodded, startled at the coldness in his eyes.

He released me like a soiled rag and picked up a small pot from the bedside table, shoving it into Azat's hands. "Treat her wounds and meet me outside. I'll muster the men. We leave at dawn."

Azat inclined his head in silent consent. When his commander left the room, he turned a condescending smirk at me. "I don't know what you said to him under that tree yesterday morning, but now he's angry at us both."

Idan hadn't told his best friend of my confession. Was that good or bad?

Azat lifted my right foot from the mattress, and I yanked it away. I realized both feet were bandaged and took a mental inventory of my body. "What happened to me?" Evidently, my overall aches masked some new wounds.

He grabbed my right ankle, jaw muscle dancing, and began unwrapping the strips of cloth.

I laid back, suddenly very aware of the pain. The last layer of cloth pulled at the wound, and I flinched. "Hold still." His words came out on a growl as he removed the bandage.

The tops of my feet and toes were scraped to the bone.

"Oh," I breathed and turned my face away, realizing Azat had dragged me last night—instead of carrying me as Idan always did. This morning, we were both paying for it. His clumsy hands bumped my wound, and I sat up, shoving him away. "Let me do it."

Glaring, he held the pot out of my reach. "You've done enough."

"You're the one who dragged me."

He leaned close, examining my lips. "I'll do with you as I please, little goddess." I turned away, terror silencing me. He laughed and smeared honey on bandages while I drowned in humiliation. Truly, any of the Scythians could do with me as he pleased, but none had assaulted me because they thought I was Tabiti. I closed my eyes and laid back, forcing myself to withstand the ministrations of a man who despised me. The cool sensation of honey-slathered bandages soothed my wounds, and I fought back tears. What if I confessed the truth to Azat now as I'd done with Idan yesterday? Would he kill me—or worse—if he knew? My conscience fought common sense.

Rough hands slid under my shoulders and knees, lifting me into a stiff-armed transport. I looked up, but Azat focused straight ahead. "Keep your wicked spells to yourself, Tabiti. Idan thinks he's immune to your powers because he has a wife and son. I have no such protection and refuse to let you trick me."

"I have no powers." It was the closest to the truth I would offer Azat.

He carried me downstairs and through the inn's front door, placing me in a cushioned and covered sedan atop a waiting camel. Idan held its reins and clicked his tongue. My two-humped beast rose to its feet, setting me high above the Scythians already waiting on their horses. As we left the last city of my ancestors, I reclined against the wool-stuffed cushions and felt guilty at the comfort. The camel's rhythmic sway rocked me to sleep, and the covered sedan sheltered me from the harsh sun.

At every respite on our four-day journey, Idan or Azat poured the foul-tasting potion down my throat, and I kept it down. Azat changed the dressing on my feet each night in the small chamber of a new two-room tent. Azat and Idan shared the tent's outer room, while I slept soundly amid the accountability of two men who no longer spoke to me or each other.

On our final full day of travel, I drank more healing potion and endured more awkward tension between the silent top soldiers. That night I lay on my reed mat, listening to squabbles in the camp erupt into violence. I felt an unwelcome sense of regret that my presence had caused division among them. Before our stop in Dan, I recalled raucous music and laughter around evening campfires.

But why should I feel regret? These men were my enemies. They caused the deaths of my son, my sister, and hundreds—thousands—of others in the city of my birth. From all I'd overheard of their campfire boasting, they'd helped plunder every city in Judah and decimated Jerusalem and Yahweh's Temple. Hate rekindled, I recounted ways to seek revenge when my body healed.

Angry voices approached our tent, and I peeked through the divider between chambers. Azat's hoarse whisper was clear. "If she were Tabiti, she would not be weak. And if she planned to give you Scythia's throne, she would willingly lead you to Nebuchadnezzar and tell you the plan of succession."

"And you know this because you've met so many gods in human form?" Idan's cynical reply set my teeth on edge. Of course, Azat would bristle.

"Ask her." Azat pointed at my curtain.

"Ask her what?"

"Ask her if she is Tabiti."

I held my breath.

"No."

Idan unrolled his mat, but Azat took a step toward the dividing curtain. "Then I'll ask her."

I pretended to be sleeping but heard a sudden scuffling, grunting, and then blows. The ground beneath me shook as two men the size of bulls rumbled steps away.

"Stop!" I screamed, standing at the open curtain. "Stop it, both of you!" Idan was on one knee, Azat's head locked under his arm. "Release him immediately. You look ridiculous."

He obeyed but shoved both fists at his hips. "Go back to your mat, woman."

Azat stood, too, nudging Idan aside. "No. Let her speak. Are you Tabiti, goddess of hearth and wealth? Swear by all you hold dear."

I glanced quickly at Idan, whose head wagged with a barely discernible warning. *Yahweh, what do I say?* I wanted to tell Azat the truth, to declare Yahweh the only true God. Abandon my lie.

But what then?

My body felt stronger with the potion and rest, but I could never escape a camp full of angry Scythians. And what happened if they discovered I'd told Idan the truth days earlier?

"Tell me." Azat's voice was softer this time, his eyes no longer narrowed with hate. "Say it."

The words sounded more like a plea than a demand. Hadn't Yahweh promised Abraham would bless all nations through him? *Yahweh, help me.* "I am not Tabiti. My name is Merari, the wife of a harp maker and servant of Yahweh, the Most High God." I turned to Idan and saw hate in his eyes. "I'm sorry."

Azat stepped away from Idan. "You knew."

Idan dropped his head, massaging the back of his neck. "No. She is Tabiti. She simply doesn't realize it."

Azat's caustic laugh made my cheeks burn. "And I'm

Papaeus. Or perhaps you're the divine father, and I can be *Targitaus*, the son?"

Idan's head shot up, his whole body rigid. "Don't patronize me. You saw the same proof I did, Azat. She called the birds to Hazor that chased away the jackals." Staring, he released a frustrated sigh. "And the scene in Jerusalem. You would believe if—"

"I know, if I'd seen the way she protected her child."

"I didn't protect him." My words escaped on a sob. I covered my mouth, trying to gain control. When I could trust my voice, I offered proof of humanity. "I couldn't protect anyone. My sister had fallen into a deep sadness. She hadn't spoken for three days. I went to a widow's house to check on her, and when I returned . . ." I couldn't say the words.

"She'd eaten part of your son." Idan spoke the truth that brought a gorge to my throat.

Swallowing hard, I turned my loathing inward. "If I were a goddess, I would have known the dark intentions of my sister's heart and would never have left my son in her care." Having rendered two war-hardened soldiers speechless, I found myself too tired to care if they thought me fraud or god. "I'm going to sleep now. Azat, kill me now or in the morning. It matters not."

I slipped through the curtain and returned to my reed mat. *Yahweh, send me to Sheol. It's what I deserve.*

CHAPTER 11

IDAN

"You will be a reproach and a taunt,
a warning and an object of horror to the nations around you
when I inflict punishment on you in anger and in wrath and with
stinging rebuke.
I the LORD have spoken."
-Ezekiel 5:15

"How else could she call thousands of birds to Hazor when jackals threatened our camp?" It was the question that kept me staring at the waning moon through the small slit in our tent flap and the only thing keeping her alive. Even Azat agreed there was something of the divine in her.

I had vowed silence to Tabiti on the floor of that little house in Jerusalem, but if she wasn't Tabiti . . . "I saw three bodies: Tabiti, a boy, and another woman. The woman's body —" I refused to describe it. "I knew only by the face still intact that it had been a woman. The boy's body had been lovingly pieced back together, dressed, and sprinkled with herbs."

"Herbs? Where did she get herbs?"

I shook my head. "That's part of the wonder. I also found this . . ." Rushing out of the tent, I made sure the sentries were distracted when I retrieved the treasure from my supply mule. Azat's face was skeptical, but when I unwrapped the exquisite harp, my wonder was reflected on his features.

"How could something so valuable survive a siege?"

"This harp and the herbs were the only things of value in her house. No clothing. No furniture. Not even dishes or tools."

Azat was shaking his head before I finished. "Why wouldn't they have sold the harp and herbs long before?"

"None of her story makes sense. She says their own god brought all this calamity because Judah worshiped other deities."

"Is that so hard to believe?" Azat's voice grew softer. "We execute any Scythian who worships gods of other nations. Is it so unthinkable that their god would require the same loyalty?"

My chest tightened at the reminder of my uncle's fate. "But what kind of god watches his temple defiled? His people butchered—by each other?"

We both sat in silence, letting the realities of war harden our weary hearts. Extended sieges brought out the worst in everyone. The soldiers and the besieged. The strong preyed on the weak, and even the noblest of character failed when survival instincts awakened. We were Scythians, warriors, mercenaries—but we were still human.

A deep sigh broke Azat's silence. "Her confession was insane, Idan. Or is she a senseless cow? We have to kill her, you know. If our men discover we've knowingly kept a Hebrew woman to ourselves, they'll think—" Another sigh. "You know what they'll think, and we'll completely lose their trust."

He was right, but I couldn't kill her. "I'm still not sure. How could a mere woman call thousands of birds with a whistle to fight off jackals?"

"Maybe birds like Hazor."

I heard the doubt in his voice. He didn't want to kill her either. "Or maybe this god of hers is actually protecting her, and he'll curse us if we harm her."

"Don't ever say that again." Azat sat up, looming over me in the darkness. "Scythians recognize no gods but our own. I'm sure your father has spies among us, and he'd kill you like he did your uncle if you admit even the possibility of other gods."

I looked away, afraid he'd see the rebellion in my eyes. My father was a fool to think Scythia's gods were alone in the heavens. "We say nothing to our men. We convince Nebuchadnezzar she's Tabiti, our chief goddess, and then ask to be released from service. He promised Judah would be Scythia's last campaign. We've done everything he asked, Azat. I'm only asking for one woman from Jerusalem to lead the Scythians home."

CHAPTER 12

MERARI, SYRIA

"The Babylonian army pursued [King Zedekiah] and overtook him in the plains of Jericho. All his soldiers were separated from him and scattered, and he was captured.
He was taken to the king of Babylon at Riblah, where sentence was pronounced on him."
-2 Kings 25:5–6

On our final day of travel to Riblah, we stopped twice before midday on the banks of the Orontos. Both times I expected to feel the effects of oleander in my water, but to my surprise, neither Idan or Azat poisoned me after last night's confession. Instead, they forced the last doses of potion down my throat.

I was strong enough now to sit up in the sedan. My swollen abdomen had decreased to a more sightly four-month baby bulge—though I hadn't slept with a man since Elon was taken captive—and both my cough and fever subsided to mere annoyance. The malaise lingered, but I attributed it to my cushioned sedan atop the camel I'd named Mara—*bitter*. The poor creature had mournful eyes, a spiteful temper, and she spit at every man who came near her.

I envied her courage.

Shading my eyes from the midday sun, I shouted ahead to Idan for the fourth time this morning. "How much farther to Riblah?"

He shrugged a shoulder, thinking that would suffice. Foolish man.

I'd rather feel a dagger than endure silence. Unwinding my head scarf, I twisted it and used it to snap Mara's rump. She surged into a gallop, pulling the reins around Idan's hand, and nearly dragged him off his prized black stallion. The troops behind us hooted and praised my resourcefulness.

My captor wasn't amused. "Why not simply ask me to kill you?" His stallion now trotted beside Mara.

Checking over my shoulder at the troops climbing the hill, I made sure I wouldn't be overheard. "Why haven't you and Azat told the others my real name?"

His eyes remained fixed ahead and I waited for his answer. What held his fascination? Following his gaze, I saw a sprawling walled city with thousands upon thousands of soldiers creating a second wall around it.

He turned to face me, fire in his eyes. "Welcome to Riblah," he said. "You are Tabiti. You will meet King Nebuchadnezzar. And you will provide a safe journey back to Scythia for my men and me."

The words felt like the dull end of a spear in my belly, each one a blow. Anger warred with despair, and all I could do was shake my head no.

As a silent threat, he pointed to a valley in the distance, and I instantly covered my mouth to stifle a cry. Like ants on the roads we'd traveled days ago flowed an endless sea of soldiers and captives—at least that's what I supposed them to be. Some on horseback, some stooped and stumbling, the sight was staggering. A countryside covered by humanity converging on Riblah to pay homage to the King of the World. My stomach rolled, and I lost my morning gruel over the side of my sedan.

While I wiped my chin, he leaned over me but kept his voice low. "Still want me to tell everyone your name is Merari, the Hebrew?" Idan's smug grin sickened me.

Glancing over my shoulder again at those coming after me, I looked down at my bandaged feet and clean hands. My new robe and head scarf. Fear silenced my conscience, and I settled back into the soft cushions, feeling filthier than a priestess after Ishtar's feast.

I'd become rather accustomed to the Scythians' appearance by now, but the Riblah valley's reaction to Idan's processional reminded me of their startling bearing. Soldiers by their campfires halted conversations to stop and stare at the muscular arms bulging from sleeveless leather tunics, belted at the waist. Tattoos told each man's life journey depicting family, battles, and faith. Intricate designs covered every visible piece of skin, except their faces, which were unique among Nebuchadnezzar's minions. Lighter skin, almond-shaped eyes, and flattened noses and cheekbones even stopped sword drills while the Scythians passed.

I noted other ethnic variations and each nation camped beneath a different standard. The Edomites bore an eagle on their flag. The Syrians camped under the symbol of a hawk. The Arabs, a palm with two crossed swords. Azat galloped from his position at rear guard, carrying the Scythian standard of a golden stag. Riding alongside Idan, they led us toward the camp's center, where one extravagant white tent posted a unique flag of its own. A strange animal I didn't recognize.

Idan lifted his fist in the air, halting the regiment about a hundred paces from the white tent. He and Azat spoke too quietly for me to hear, but whatever was said seemed to please Azat. He rode back to his men, falling in line with the first row, and faced the fine tent. Idan dismounted and offered his reins to a stable boy, tapping my camel's shoulder. Mara buckled her knees and seemed content to rest, but I politely declined when Idan offered his hand.

"You go ahead. I'll wait with your men."

I detected a faint smile. "Get off the camel, *Tabiti*."

I glanced over my shoulder at Azat. He lifted a brow like my ima's silent, *Don't make me use the rod.* In Azat's case, it was more likely to be his dagger. I accepted Idan's hand and stepped out of the sedan onto Riblah's grassy carpet.

He laced my arm around his, and leaned over slightly, keeping his voice low. "You are dressed as a Scythian goddess. Act like one."

How did a Scythian goddess act? I decided to pose a safer question and pointed at the flag on the white tent. "What is that creature?"

"It's the Sirrush, the representation of Nebuchadnezzar's patron god, Marduk. Part lion, part dragon, part eagle and snake."

"It's ugly."

He coughed, masking a grin. "Spoken like a Scythian goddess but not likely to win Nebuchadnezzar's favor." He stopped walking and held my gaze. "We get one chance to convince him you're Tabiti. My future hangs in the balance—as does your life."

"But I don't want to live in Scythia." The words were out before I could stop them.

His eyes widened, showing the same surprise I felt, but his

cheeks quickly shaded crimson. His wrath was preempted, however, by the approach of pounding hooves. Idan pulled me off the path, uttering a Scythian curse as horsemen in Babylonian armor passed us.

I waved away a cloud of dust, and he grabbed my hand. "Can you run?" I gave half a nod, and he flew. I could barely keep pace, gasping for breath by the time we arrived at the white tent.

The lead rider disappeared into the tent shouting, "We've captured King Zedekiah!"

Idan skidded to a halt and stood like a statue. Panting like one of the horses around us, he released my hand, his clenching into tight fists. I couldn't decide if it was safer to move toward him or closer to the soldiers on horseback. What did news of Zedekiah's capture mean to the crown prince of Scythia?

Without warning, he grabbed my arm and fairly dragged me back toward his troops. "I'll speak with Nebuchadnezzar tomorrow or maybe next—"

"Prince Idanthyrsus!" A bass voice rattled my chest, sending a chill down my spine.

Idan's leather boot slipped on the grass, and his fingers bit into my arm. He whispered while turning us around. "Don't say a word." His hand moved to my shoulder, forcing me into a bow as deep as his. "Great and mighty King of the World, I am honored to hear you speak my full name."

I heard the swish of footsteps on grass and saw large, brown feet in bejeweled sandals stop a single pace away. "Why are you running like a desert hare in the opposite direction?" King Nebuchadnezzar tipped up my chin. "And who is this wilted flower?"

I stared into the face of evil. He was stunning. Gleaming

white teeth peeked between an oiled and curled black beard. Black eyes danced over my form with the confidence of a man who had never been denied. Purple robe. Gold wrist bands. Jeweled belt.

Idan stood tall, matching Nebuchadnezzar's height, appearing every bit as strong. "I came to make introductions, but when I heard the good news of Zedekiah's capture, I realized my business could wait until we celebrate your great victory." He bowed again as if preparing to leave, but Nebuchadnezzar snared my arm.

"Nonsense. I'd like to meet your woman. We have time before the rebels arrive." Nebuchadnezzar started back to his tent, dragging me with him.

Casting a pleading glance over my shoulder, I saw pink splotches turn crimson on Idan's neck. My legs turned to water, knowing that what awaited me in the tent would make a Scythian blush.

CHAPTER 13

IDAN

"I will set my face against them and make them an example and a
byword . . .
Then you will know that I am the LORD."
-Ezekiel 14:8

When General Nebuzaradan and his troops rode into camp like madmen, I knew he'd likely tell the king my regiment left Jerusalem without securing his permission. I had hoped to arrive in Riblah before the general had time to poison the king against me. My regiment left to protect my prized goddess—while the Judean king scampered like a rat through Jerusalem's underground tunnels.

It was another on a growing list of my mistakes on this campaign.

"May King Nebuchadnezzar live forever." I heard running footfalls behind me and drew my dagger.

The king turned, holding his blade at Tabiti's throat. Azat skidded to a stop, and fell to both knees, hands extended before him. "May I guard the goddess while you speak with my prince?"

An amused smile lit Nebuchadnezzar's hard features. "*The goddess*, you say? Now I'm even more interested in this wilted flower." He pulled her into the tent, and I bent to growl at my captain.

"Stay with the men and leave diplomacy to me." I rushed inside and found Nebuchadnezzar sitting on an elevated ebony throne covered with furs and animal skins.

His six top commanders taunted Tabiti, laughing and prodding her with their spear handles like a mule in their stables. I met the king's gaze, and he raised an eyebrow as if playing a game. My move.

While the commanders focused on Tabiti, I slipped into the shadowy corners. Staying low, I roared into three commanders, tackling them before the others knew it. Amid the confusion, I flung Tabiti aside and disarmed the other three, inflicting only minor wounds.

"Well done." Nebuchadnezzar held Tabiti against his chest, dagger again poised at her throat. She trembled but didn't whimper—not even when he leaned down and kissed her cheek. "Please, Prince Idan, introduce me to the *goddess* who caused you to abandon your duties in Jerusalem."

General Nebuzaradan, one of three I'd tackled, extended his hand, demanding my dagger. Refusing to give up my only weapon, I glared at the king, who drew his blade gently across Tabiti's throat.

At the first sign of blood, I cried out, "No!" and offered up my weapon.

Nebuzaradan backhanded me. "You're a fool."

"Enough!" The king lowered the dagger and pressed Tabiti

to the floor beside his throne. "Your goddess will sit with me while you explain yourself, Scythian."

Forcing calm, I met her gaze as she wiped the small wound with her scarf. She offered a weak smile and a nod, giving me confidence to continue. "King Nebuchadnezzar, may I introduce Tabiti, Scythia's mother goddess, protector of hearth and wealth, purity and fidelity."

He grabbed her chin roughly, turning her face side to side. "Your goddess appears very Hebrew."

She remained silent—as I'd instructed her. I must convince Babylon's king now. "When I entered a home in the lower city, I saw proof that she had healed a dead boy. I secreted her to my tent and returned to help my regiment finish sweeping the southern city." I cast a loathing glare on General Nebuzaradan. "Upon completion of our mission, we noticed increasing chaos in the upper city. Fearing an enemy uprising, my regiment charged up the hill to assist but stopped when we saw Babylonian regiments destroying Jerusalem's temple. A clear violation of your orders, my king."

Noting the general's growing unease, I was certain triumph was imminent. "Since your chief wise man—Belteshazzar—cautioned us to reverence Yahweh's temple and you, great king, commanded orderly disassembly, my regiment followed *your* orders above the general's and returned to camp. In absolute obedience, we hoped to escape retribution from you or the Hebrews' powerful god."

Nebuchadnezzar's eyes aimed daggers at his general. "You failed to mention the disorder at the temple. I can't afford the ire of Belteshazzar's god."

"I saw no reason to alarm you, my king." Nebuzaradan bowed and remained in the penitent pose. "Your instructions were to find the prophet Jeremiah, care for him, and carefully dismantle the valuables from Yahweh's temple in order to transport them to Babylon." He lifted his head. "The prophet Jeremiah has been placed in the care of the newly-appointed governor, Gedaliah. Three regiments remain in Jerusalem to catalog the temple items, which will arrive in Riblah within the week. King Zedekiah, his officials, and his family have been captured and will arrive shortly to receive your judgment."

He cast a fleeting sneer in my direction. "Prince Idan exaggerates to shift attention from his own treachery. His regiment ignored the chain of command. They are cowards who deserted their fellow *Scythians*, leaving the other three thousand of King Saulius' men in Jerusalem under my command." The general pointed at me with a gold-ringed, stubby finger. "His entire regiment should be executed."

I slapped his finger out of my face. "I left my three thousand Scythians because we're *not* cowards, you ignorant cow—"

"Silence!" Nebuchadnezzar shouted.

I bowed to one knee, as did the general when he saw my deference. In a moment of excruciating silence, the sounds of more horses and footsteps outside was followed by a rustling of the tent flap. I didn't dare turn to see who entered.

"What?" the king growled.

"The rebels have arrived and await your judgment."

I rose in time to see Nebuchadnezzar's eyes narrow at me. "Prince Idan, you left Jerusalem without the permission of your commanding officer." He shifted his ire to the general. "And you disregarded Belteshazzar's warnings and disobeyed my direct command to treat Yahweh's temple with care." He grabbed Tabiti's arm and pulled her alongside him, halting between us. "You will both pay close attention to how I deal with Zedekiah, a man under my authority who refused to follow instructions. And we'll see how a goddess responds to greatness." He proceeded out of the tent, dragging Tabiti with him.

CHAPTER 14

MERARI

*"They killed the sons of Zedekiah before his eyes.
Then they put out his eyes, bound him with bronze shackles
and took him to Babylon." -*2 Kings 25:7

ebuchadnezzar dragged me from the tent and into the waiting circle of judgment. Jeering soldiers surrounded at least a hundred half-naked, beaten, and starving men. All shackled in bronze chains. King Zedekiah was among them, and I recognized a few other officials who had purchased harps from Elon or me. But there was one face I could never forget . . .

Jehukal.

The flirty nobleman who harassed me every day in the market now cowered among the captives. Bloodied and stripped to his tunic, he was half the man I'd seen strolling through Jerusalem's streets. I blinked away tears, refusing to cry for a man I didn't even like. But no one deserved this.

"Where are the wives and children?" Nebuchadnezzar roared and then looked down at me, grinning. He reminded me of a serpent. I waited for a forked tongue to slither between his lips. "Surely, the goddess Tabiti cares nothing about the death of a few Jews."

Jews? My mind reeled, the strange term tumbling like a pebble in an empty basket. We were Yahweh's chosen. Hebrews. Israelites. Judeans. But Jews?

The king raised his voice again. "Bring me King Zedekiah, his wives, and his sons!"

My knees weakened. My senses soared. Sounds, smells, and sights overwhelmed, knocking me to the ground. The king's brown hand seized my arm, his musky odor overpowering.

Idan's face was close. "Tabiti, are you well?"

The ground beneath felt as if it was spinning, and I braced myself, trying to look up. Soldiers' armor caught the glint of sunshine. So many shapes and types of armor in the circle of brutes. Nations of the world, assembled against my people.

Water splashed my face, startling me to reality. "I wouldn't want you to miss the victory celebration." Nebuchadnezzar threw an empty clay cup to the ground and turned to King Zedekiah. "I set you on Judah's throne, protected you from marauding nations, and still you conspired with Pharaoh Hophra. Your relative, a man you would know as Daniel ben Johanan, is chief of my wise men. He tells me your demise is judgment from your god and I'm the instrument of wrath in Yahweh's hand." He placed his dagger under Zedekiah's eye. "Do you believe I'm your god's weapon of destruction?"

Zedekiah swallowed hard. "I believe whatever you say."

"Of course you do." Eyes locked on Zedekiah's, he ground out the words, "Should I kill your family because you're a traitor or because your god told me to do so?"

"Kill me, my king. Not my sons."

Nebuchadnezzar withdrew his blade and looked over the

rest of the captives. "But what lesson would my soldiers learn if I killed only you, Zedekiah?" He raised his hand, motioning to his men. "Arrange the officials with their families according to rank. We'll kill them slowly."

I hid my face, while the barbarians began their war games, but a soldier pushed my hands away. Idan shoved him but without his dagger, he was helpless to protect himself or me.

"Stop!" Nebuchadnezzar shouted, and every living thing stilled. He crouched beside me and whispered, "You will watch every moment of Yahweh's wrath, or you will see your Scythian prince in chains with the Jews." He smiled up at Idan, having spoken loud enough for him to hear, and then stood and shouted at his soldiers. "Prove you are the victors!"

I set my gaze on the captives and found Jehukal watching me. A woman stood beside him. His wife, no doubt, with an expression hard as flint. If she could stare, I could stare. Barely blinking. Never flinching. Hardly breathing. All afternoon I watched. By dusk, the only ones left to kill were Zedekiah, two of his sons, three officials, and their wives. Jehukal and his wife were among them, their eyes now glazed and empty.

"I'll finish the evening with final verdicts on Judah's highest officials, my general, and Scythia's crown prince." The circle collapsed as blood-covered soldiers crowded nearer. Azat shouldered his way to the front directly opposite us, exchanging a nod with Idan. I searched the circle, looking for the rest of their regiment, and found them sprinkled throughout. I glanced up at Idan, questioning, but his subtle warning returned my eyes forward.

Nebuchadnezzar extended his hand to me, and I stood. When he led me toward Zedekiah and Jehukal, I pulled my hand away, stopping so abruptly Idan bumped into me.

The king extended his hand again. "You will come."

His hand waited there like the abyss. I placed my hand in it and was swallowed up by the King of the World. Numbly I followed, and he halted before Judah's broken king. "You worship many gods, do you not, Zedekiah?"

"Yes, I . . . I suppose I—"

"Have you ever heard of the Scythian goddess, Tabiti?"

"No, my king. Never." I felt Jehukal's stare, but tried to focus on Nebuchadnezzar's words.

He scratched his oiled beard, feigning confusion. "Scythia's crown prince thinks his goddess lived in Jerusalem, and you never knew she was there? That troubles me, Zedekiah."

In a single step, he blocked me from all others, towering over me with his imposing presence. "You will tell me who you are, or I will make your life worse than death."

I stared into the eyes of evil and shuddered. After the tortures I'd seen today, I knew death was a gift, and his threat was real. Without considering any consequence but my own, I inhaled my last thread of courage and exhaled the truth.

"My name is Merari. I'm a Hebrew woman from Jerusalem's lower city, a harp-maker's wife, but now a harp maker myself, because you took my husband to Babylon eleven years ago. I was unconscious when Prince Idan found me, but I mumbled a name he thought was Tabiti. When I woke, I let the ruse continue in hopes Yahweh would somehow reunite me with my husband when I reached Babylon." My words had spilled out like wine on a white robe, and the king's eyes widened with each revelation.

In those harrowing moments of silence, the king's intermittent glances from Idan and then back to me, I was certain my life was over. Then King Nebuchadnezzar burst into a fit of laughter.

Slowly, tentatively at first, others joined him, and then the whole circle of soldiers fell into uproarious hysteria. I dared a glance at Idan and saw crimson splotches rising on his neck. I bowed my head, surprisingly saddened for him but relieved to have spoken truth—whatever the outcome.

Nebuchadnezzar wiped tears, letting his laughter wind down. "Prince Idan, it appears you and your men have been duped by a lovesick harp-maker's wife."

Idan stepped forward and knelt, head bowed. "I realize it sounds ludicrous, my king, but if you will hear me out. I—"

"I will *not!*" Nebuchadnezzar's anger erupted, silencing the folly. "You acted independently of your commander and abandoned your post. For this you will continue in my service until you have placed all of Judah's captives in Babylon. Then—and only then, Prince Idanthyrsus—do I give you and your Scythians permission to return home."

I fell to my knees and kissed the king's filthy feet. "Please, don't punish Idan because of me." Looking up, I found his brow furrowed. At least he was listening. "He truly believed I was his goddess. He's a good man, who cared for my wounds and my illness, and he has a wife and son waiting for him. Please, let him go."

Nebuchadnezzar's rough, callused hand scraped my cheek. "You're quite captivating, little harp maker. Perhaps you're worth saving."

I sagged to my side, and Idan bent to help me, but the king's guards pulled him away from me. The circle of soldiers shouted for blood, and a slow, wicked grin bloomed on General Nebuzaradan's face.

The king lifted his hand, quieting the hecklers. "I'll finish the administrative details before celebrating the Jews' final verdicts. General Nebuzaradan . . ." The man looked startled but quickly knelt before the king. "You will return to Jerusalem and oversee the cataloguing of Temple treasures, the transfer of all captives to Riblah, and the complete destruction of the city. Reassure the prophet Jeremiah he is welcome in Babylon or he may remain in Jerusalem, but I ask for his prayers to the Hebrew God on my behalf in return. You will then escort the treasure back here to Riblah in an orderly caravan. I will see you within four weeks. Understood?"

Nebuzaradan lifted his head and pounded his fist over his heart. "Yes, my king."

The king leaned forward, lowering his voice. "If your careless command of my troops has angered Belteshazzar's god, I will make you wish—"

"The Scythian is lying. I never lost contro—"

"You've proven yourself unable to command the Scythians." This, Nebuchadnezzar shouted for all to hear. "Prince Idan is no longer under your command. Return to your tent, and leave for Jerusalem at dawn." Nebuzaradan shot a burning stare at Idan but swallowed his words and stalked away.

Angry and tense, the king's attention now turned to Idan and me. "Kneel before me, both of you." We hurried to obey, heads bowed. "Prince Idan, you will oversee troops here in camp, organize captives as they arrive, and help assign them to cities in Babylon."

I turned to see if he was angry at the verdict or anxious about mine. Our eyes met for only a moment before the king continued. "I will spare your pretty little Jewess and allow one of the officials' wives to become her handmaid. She speaks and acts like deity, so deity she'll become—at least until she arrives in Babylon."

The soldiers jeered and cajoled, disappointed at the king's mercy. He addressed the officials' wives at the end of the captive line. "You have a choice, ladies. Die now with your

BY THE WATERS OF BABYLON

husbands and children or live and serve the harp maker. Step forward if you'd like to live."

Jehukal's wife was the only volunteer, and Nebuchadnezzar looked at me like a hungry lion. "I've made you a goddess. What will you give me in return?"

Heart pounding in my ears, the words escaped before approved by wisdom. "If you find a harp, I'll play it for you."

PART II

*"The word of the L*ORD *came to [Ezekiel]:*
'Son of man, if a country sins against me by being unfaithful
and I stretch out my hand against it to cut off its food supply and
send famine upon it
and kill its people and their animals, even if these three men
—Noah, Daniel, and Job—
were in it, they could save only themselves by their righteousness . . .
Or if I send wild beasts through that country and they leave it
childless
and it becomes desolate so that no one can pass through it because of
the beasts . . .
even if these three men were in it, they could not save their own sons
or daughters.
They alone would be saved, but the land would be desolate.
Or if I bring a sword against that country . . . even if these three men
were in it,

they could not save their own sons or daughters. They alone would
be saved.
Or if I send a plague into that land . . . even if Noah, Daniel and Job
were in it,
they could save neither son nor daughter.
They would save only themselves by their righteousness . . .
How much worse will it be when I send against Jerusalem my four
dreadful judgments
—sword and famine and wild beasts and plague—
to kill its men and their animals! Yet there will be some survivors . . .
and when you see their conduct and their actions,
you will be consoled regarding the disaster I have brought on
Jerusalem . . .
for you will know that I have done nothing in it without cause."
-Ezekiel 14:12–23

CHAPTER 15

IDAN - THREE WEEKS LATER

*"[Jeremiah] took the cup [of wrath] from the LORD's hand and made
all the nations . . . drink it: Jerusalem and the towns of Judah, its
kings and officials . . .
Pharaoh king of Egypt . . . all the kings of Uz; all the kings of the
Philistines . . .
Edom, Moab and Ammon . . . all the kings of Tyre and Sidon;
the kings of the coastlands across the sea;
Dedan, Tema, Buz and all who are in distant places;
all the kings of Arabia and all the kings of the foreign people who live
in the wilderness;
all the kings of Zimri, Elam and Media; and all the kings of
the north,
near and far, one after the other—all the kingdoms on the face of
the earth."*
-Jeremiah 25:17–26

Seeing the bleeding had stopped, I pulled the strip of linen from the cut on my forearm. This morning's attack left another of General Nebuzaradan's spies injured and humiliated. His men lurked behind every date palm and acacia tree to prove me disloyal to the three thousand Scythian brothers I'd left to fight with the general in Jerusalem. But my men knew better. Three weeks in Riblah, and I'd passed Nebuzaradan's every attempt to discredit me. Instead, his constant tests had proven both my skill and determination to my men. The general was a fool.

But Scythians weren't made for lounging in one place. My 3,100 troops had bickered and fought all day. Dusk descending, I squeezed the back of my neck and considered calling for one of the camp harlots to massage my aching muscles. Stopping at the tent flap, I added another pebble to our daily count. Twenty-one. We needed to get back on the road.

I pushed open the flap. "Azat! Merari!" Empty. I kicked the cold stones around the cookfire. My belly growled, fueling my anger and loosening my tongue. "If she'd been a goddess, she could have conjured up our evening meals." It was the second time in a week I would eat dried meat and leftover bread.

I pawed through some baskets to find something edible and then sat cross-legged until my three stragglers appeared, shadows long in the setting sun. I met Azat before he reached the tent's awning. "Merari doesn't need both you and the slave to guard her while she plays for the king."

"I'm not a slave!"

Back-handing the old cow, I silenced her familiar objection.

"Stop!" Merari stepped between us, flinching as if I might hit her.

But who could beat the harp player for the king—even if she had delayed my plan to take Scythia's throne. "Why defend a servant who hates you and refuses to obey?"

Three weeks of the king's provisions had pinked her cheeks

and sharpened her tongue. "Slave or free, no one should be beaten like an animal."

The slave crossed her arms over an ample bosom. "Why not let them kill me?"

Merari whirled on her. "Hush, Helah. Start the fire."

Azat nodded at the old woman, eyebrows raised with a silent, *This is why I must take both.* The old cow would get herself killed with that impudent tongue, and Merari believed herself responsible for the slave. I kicked a couple of baskets toward the women. "Surely, you can fix something for tonight's meal. It's a wonder your husbands didn't starve . . ." My careless words died, when I remembered too late that barely a month ago, they *were* starving in a siege I inflicted.

Azat grabbed my arm and pulled me into the tent, saving me from humiliation. I dug the heels of my hands into my eyes and rolled onto my mat. "Why do I always say the wrong thing to that woman?"

He reached for a pitcher and splashed his arms with water. "Every man she meets stumbles over his words and shoves someone out of the way to get closer. I had to take down two enthusiastic Edomites today." His expression clouded. "The king hasn't defiled her—yet."

I sat up, noting the fervor with which he dried his arms and hands. "Do you expect him to take her?"

Azat's hands stilled, back turned to me. "Not if he expects to live." He tossed the cloth aside and turned to leave.

"Azat!" I lunged and caught his arm. "Tell me you won't get yourself killed." Our first day in Riblah, he'd scattered our regiment among the circle of celebration and planned a coordinated attack if Nebuchadnezzar ordered my execution. Brave. Noble. But suicide, and he knew it. "Talk to me, brother."

Azat scrubbed his head, leaving his hair tousled, and let me tug him toward our mats. We sat opposite each other. "I believe Nebuchadnezzar is too frightened of Merari's god to touch her." His eyes were so intense, they nearly burned me. "The King of the World is afraid, Idan. So, no. I wouldn't kill King Nebuchadnezzar if he touched Merari. I don't think I'd have to. Some of the stories about Yahweh they've told each other—especially the stories about this Belteshazzar, whose Hebrew name is Daniel . . ." He let his words sink in and then raked his fingers through his hair again. "If Yahweh is as powerful as Merari says—as powerful as Nebuchadnezzar believes—we should be afraid, Idan."

"No!" I glanced out the slender tent opening and saw the women talking quietly. "I will warn you as you warned me. You must never let anyone think you believe in another god—"

"I know," he said, "but the stories, Idan. You should hear—"

"That's all they are."

"No! Listen to me." He grabbed my face. "King Nebuchadnezzar sentenced three Jews to execution by fire and threw them into a smelting furnace on the plain of Dura. His own soldiers were burned up from the intense heat while throwing the Jews into the fire, but the Hebrew god stood inside a smelting furnace and protected the three men."

"Impossible," I said. "He's mocking you."

"No! He said when he called the Jews out, they walked from the furnace and bowed before him without being singed or even the scent of smoke on their clothing."

I peered again out the slender opening of our tent and caught Merari's silhouette in the fire's glow. If her god was so powerful, why had he allowed his temple and patron city to be destroyed?

A strange howl in the distance was joined immediately by a shriek. Terror erupted in the camp.

"Get your axe, Azat!" We rushed out of the tent as Merari and the old cow screamed and ran in.

I stood in wonder, watching a motley mix of beasts—hyenas, jackals, wolves, and even brown bears—flow from the hills as if a mighty hand had released them from a bursting pen.

Azat swung his axe at my head. I ducked, and a jackal rolled to the ground in two pieces. I released a war cry, and my friend joined me. We dashed into the skirmish. Captives cowered in clusters without weapons, and the beasts attacked only soldiers with swords and axes. The battle was fierce.

The animals came in waves. Just when we believed they'd retreated, more snarling invaders leapt from the darkness and another army of predators attacked the king's troops. Weapons glinted in moonlight, slashing fur and bone. At dawn, beasts finally receded into shadows and weary men pondered our unprecedented foe.

As camp commander, it fell to me to compile the dead and wounded. Some were reported missing, dragged into the hills, their distant screams eerie in dawn's haze. Commanders from each nation came to report their losses under the canopy of our tent. Grim-faced and dazed, some had lost dozens, others hundreds.

A hand on my shoulder made me flinch. "*Shh*, it's just me." Merari set a cup of watered wine on the ground beside me.

"There's evil in the air." I shivered and reached for the cup, glancing at her over the rim as I drank. Was that a faint smile? "You think it's funny so many men lost their lives?"

Her eyes sparked with controlled fury, her voice low but strong. "It's neither funny, nor evil. It's Yahweh who sent beasts into camp last night. Our prophet foretold His wrath would be poured out on the nations who destroyed Jerusalem." She stepped toward the tent but hesitated, her back still turned. "Perhaps Yahweh has revealed Himself to you—spared you—so you can share Him with your people."

I took another swig. "Scythians don't worship foreign gods." I pointed to the Jewish captives, who now served their wounded captors. "Look what happened when your people turned against their god. What good could come if I turned against mine?"

"Your gods were created by men, Idan. My God *created* men."

She disappeared into the tent before I could reply, and a chill worked up my spine. Merari had grown stronger in both body and spirit. I still felt whispers of the divine in her and feared this new truth more than the first lie. What if her god was real? What if Yahweh was responsible for the 137 dead and 789 wounded soldiers, for sending the mysterious beasts in the dark of night? Would they come again when the sun set?

I couldn't risk another attack tonight. "Azat!" He emerged from the tent as I stood. "I'm going to urge the king to strike camp immediately. We must leave for Babylon."

CHAPTER 16

MERARI, HAMATH IN SYRIA

"You who have escaped the sword, leave and do not linger!
Remember the LORD in a distant land, and call to mind Jerusalem."
-Jeremiah 51:50

elah stood with feet planted and hands on hips in the small section of the double tent, while I scurried around her to pack our meager belongings.

"You could help," I suggested.

"Why pack? I'm not leaving."

I rolled my eyes and bent to retrieve a twig I used to comb my hair. Nebuchadnezzar threatened to sheer my head bald if we didn't remove the mats from it, but he neglected to provide a comb. In the three weeks since Helah had seen her husband tortured and murdered, combing my hair with this twig had been the only time she'd shared her pain. She was all brambles and thorns outside but raw and grieving inside.

I reached for her hand, but she pulled away as if I was leprous. "I'm not a child. I don't need your pity."

"Then *you* pack the rest and load it on the camel." I stomped out of the tent and immediately regretted it.

Idan stood in his adjoining chamber, grinning. "We could leave her here to meet the jackals and hyenas tonight."

"I'm staying," Helah shouted from behind the dividing curtain.

Idan laughed, but I was still fuming. "Don't encourage her defiance."

"You must beat her."

"I won't."

"There are plenty of other Jewish women in camp now, and more will arrive when General Nebuzaradan catches up on our way to Babylon." He unsheathed his dagger, a distinct and terrifying sound. "This old cow should be slaughtered."

"I'm packing!" Helah shouted from beyond the curtain.

I blocked Idan's path, and he put away his dagger. "If she doesn't work, she doesn't live."

He left the tent to oversee the corralling of captives. Because the Scythians were nomads and efficient travelers, all 3,100 warriors were packed and ready to escort the captives well before midday. Helah helped me finish packing our meager belongings, and I climbed into my cushioned sedan atop Mara shortly after, feeling overwhelmingly guilty. Over three thousand of my people were rousted from their flimsy pine-branch shelters, many still in the throes of starvation and plague, to begin a month-long journey on foot.

"They can barely stand," I said to Idan. "How do you expect them to march all the way to Babylon?"

"Some will die, it's true, but the will to live is strong." He shaded his eyes from the morning sun. "You, above all people, should know this, *Tabiti*."

My desire to help was equally compelling. For the next

three days, Helah and I walked among the captives, choosing the weakest or sickest to ride in Mara's sedan. My camel sometimes carried as many as five adults.

Idan protested. "That sedan was built for two people. Three at the most."

"Skin and bone weigh half as much," I said, helping a little girl into her mother's arms. He growled and prodded his stallion into a gallop.

Each night, after a hearty meal prepared by his cooks, Nebuchadnezzar summoned me to play a borrowed harp. He said it belonged to one of his men, but Elon's signature was etched into the base. It was a Jewish harp, one from a captive's belongings. With a little tuning, it sang almost as brightly as my wedding harp—the one lost to me in Jerusalem. It had been the only treasure I'd saved during the siege, the only earthly possession I mourned.

"Are you ready?" Azat's hand on my shoulder interrupted my brooding.

Without answer, I left the fire, went into our tent, and retrieved the borrowed harp. On this, our fourth night of travel, the Scythians camped amid the king's guard just outside the walled city of Hamath. Larger than Riblah, it was farther from the hills and wild beasts, but Idan still stationed twice the guards.

I startled at a noise behind me. Turning, I found Azat in the tiny space Helah and I shared. I stepped back, trapped against the tent's canvas. "Get out."

Lifting his hands, he stepped closer. "I won't hurt you."

"Stop, or I'll scream." I pressed my hand against his chest and felt his heart pounding.

He dropped his hands and lowered his voice to a whisper. "I need to know . . . if you want me to stop the king if he attempts to . . . If he tries to . . ." He shrugged and raised his brows like a doe-eyed boy.

Both touched and humiliated, I covered my flaming cheeks. "King Nebuchadnezzar would not . . . He doesn't think of me that way . . . He loves his wife!"

Azat took a single step back and made no attempt to hide a grin. "I assure you, Mistress Merari, now that your curves have returned, every man in camp thinks of you that way. Wife or no wife."

"Uuuhhh!" Humiliation complete, I turned my back. "Get out!"

But there was no flutter of the curtain or retreating footsteps. "You haven't answered my question, Merari. Do you wish me to stop the king if he sets upon you?"

Azat's voice held the tenderness of a friend, and I faced the *mighty little man*—as Idan called him—who could never save me from a king's advances or his six royal bodyguards. "No, Azat. I can't allow you to intervene."

His jaw muscle danced, eyes searching mine. "Are you hoping to become his mistress?"

"Oh!" Chuckling nervously, I pressed my hands against my forehead. "Absolutely not!" His features relaxed, though I wasn't sure why. Why did it matter to a Scythian warrior if Babylon's king took a Hebrew concubine?

Helah squeezed into the small space, pressing Azat closer. She eyed him like a toad in her laundry basket. "Why are you standing on my sleeping mat? Get out."

Azat's fingers brushed my hand before he elbowed Helah out of the way. "The king awaits his harp player. Let's go, Merari."

I stood frozen. Had he meant to touch me? He joked and

talked with Idan outside the curtain as if nothing at all had happened.

Helah picked up the harp. "Come. You heard him."

My legs moved like wooden sticks, and I wasn't sure which I feared more. Advances from the King of Babylon or a new undercurrent of emotion from my Scythian guard.

CHAPTER 17

MERARI, ALEPPO IN SYRIA

"Therefore this is what the LORD says:
You have not obeyed me; you have not proclaimed freedom to your
own people.
So I now proclaim 'freedom' for you, declares the LORD—
'freedom' to fall by the sword, plague and famine.
I will make you abhorrent to all the kingdoms of the earth."
-Jeremiah 34:17

"When is it my turn on that blasted camel?" Helah leaned heavily on her walking stick, her grousing a hoarse whisper on our fifth day of travel.

I had no strength to answer. The woman leaning on me was barely conscious, but my camel's sedan was already full of plague victims. While in Hamath, I'd coerced the king to purchase the same tea Idan had given me, but we used the last of it yesterday. Some grew stronger and ate well. Some even played songs of Zion on instruments they'd brought from home; strumming harps, clanging timbrels, beating drums. Looking over my shoulder at the train of captives, soldiers, wagons, horses, donkeys, and camels, I despaired of ever sleeping under a roof again.

Stumbling, I was on the ground before I realized I'd fallen. The woman with me fell, too, moaning as she rolled down a small incline. I reached for her but not quick enough to catch her and couldn't get to my knees. Rough hands grabbed my ribs. I cried out and fell hard to the rocky ground.

"Merari." Azat knelt over me, shaking my shoulders. "Merari?"

"Help me stand." It was a whisper.

Idan stood over his shoulder. "Get the invalids off her camel and put her back in the sedan. If she dies now, Nebuchadnezzar will cut us all into pieces."

I wanted to protest but couldn't gather the strength. Azat lifted me gently, and I was surprised at how secure his arms felt. "Thank you for not dragging me." His chest rumbled with a chuckle. Though only a head taller than me, he was indeed a mighty man.

The caravan waited long enough to evict the five captives from my sedan and place me there. Three of the five were already dead, and the other two would die where we left them. I mourned each one though I didn't know them, weeping while I lay on the wretched, filthy cushions. Between tears, I slept. Azat forced me to eat and drink whenever the caravan stopped. He even shared his water with Helah who now joined me in the sedan.

By dusk that day, a scout announced the city of Aleppo lay on the other side of the next hill. Thankfully, the king was too tired for his harp player that evening. Helah and I fixed a quick meal of warm bread, hard cheese, and dried figs while the men set up our tent. We all ate quickly. I cleaned the dishes; Helah went to the river for fresh water. I don't know when she returned. I'd already fallen into a dreamless sleep.

The next morning, I woke to a strange mewling sound. Low at first, growing in intensity. Lifting my head, I realized it was Helah. Her back to me, she was shaking in the dim light of dawn.

I crawled closer and laid my hand on her shoulder. "Can I help?"

This time, she didn't pull away. "Can you kill King Nebuchadnezzar and every man outside our tent?"

So much for reasoning. "No, but I can assure you that Yahweh will punish those who delight in doing us harm."

"Yahweh?" She sat up and shoved me away. "How dare you speak to me of Yahweh? He is a legend of prophets to frighten the masses. I'm forced to listen to that barbarous king's claims of him while you play your harp, but I am not your slave, and I won't listen to you!"

"No, Helah. You're not my slave, but—"

A huge hand reached through the dividing curtain and grabbed Helah by the hair, dragging her backward into the main room of the tent.

Panic seized me. "No, Idan! Don't hurt her. Please!" I scrambled into the main room, following Helah's whimpering.

Idan held her back against his chest, dagger pressed to her throat. "Why shouldn't I kill her, Merari? She's a terrible slave and a miserable woman. If I slit her throat, she'll feel better. You'll feel better. Azat and I will most certainly feel better."

"She's Yahweh's child." The words erupted from somewhere unknown, but our captor's face went as pale as the moonlight.

He released her, and Helah sagged to the floor, crawling back to me. I knelt, pulling her into my arms, rocking as she wept the kind of tears I'd shed yesterday for only Mara to hear.

Idan crouched beside us. "What do you mean, she's 'Yahweh's child'?" He studied Helah, lips curved in disdain. "Our mother goddess bore four children—lesser gods but still powerful. None of them piteous like her."

I closed my eyes, reminding myself to be cautious but truthful. "Helah is human as we are. Yahweh is the only God, the lone Creator of all things. But He chose Abraham of the Chaldeans and all his descendants to preserve His truth for the whole world's blessing. My cousin Jeremiah taught us that all who believe with faith like Abraham's become Yahweh's adopted children."

Idan stepped back with a strange hesitancy. "Your cousin Jeremiah. Was he the shaman? The *prophet* Jeremiah?"

"How do you know that?" My confusion gave way to dread when Idan massaged the back of his neck. "I know only that Zedekiah held him prisoner in the courtyard of the guard during the siege. Is he alive?"

Idan took another step back. "Do you have his powers?" Now both he and Azat stared as if Tabiti were reborn.

"I have no magical powers and neither do Yahweh's prophets. Now, please . . ." Frustration laced my tone. "Tell me what you know."

With a glint of metal and a whirl of strength, Helah was out of my arms and Idan's dagger was poised beneath my eye.

Azat stood over us. "Idan, no."

"Your cousin is a free man in the care of Jerusalem's new governor. But you, Merari . . . You're a captive. Why is Yahweh justified for killing his *children* but I'm restrained from killing you?"

Barely breathing, I uttered the only truth I knew. "Because He is God and you are not."

"Aaaahhhh!" He threw his dagger into the center post and

cursed, stomping out of the tent. "I should have killed her in Jerusalem!"

Azat grinned at me. "He liked you better as Tabiti." He started out of the tent but glanced over his shoulder. "I like you as Merari."

When the tent flap closed behind him, a soft touch brushed my arm. "Thank you." Helah lay shaking beside me. "I don't hate you, Merari, but I'll never understand how you can defend a god who kills women and children. Innocent people. Good people."

My heart ached that Yahweh was a stranger to her. I tucked a few black and silver strands behind her ear. "When compared to God's perfect love, His unblemished goodness, no one is innocent, Helah. Our hearts are filthy rags when compared to His robes of white."

"But what about the children?" Her voice cracked, and she hid her face.

I bent over her, my tears wetting her back, remembering my own precious boy. When I could speak, a piece of my story was given as pledge. "I lost my only son in the siege, Helah. He was killed by a sin-sickened heart, but is with Yahweh now in perfect peace."

She lifted her head, eyes wide. "I didn't know, Merari. I'm sorry. Jehukal and I never had children."

I nodded, grateful she didn't know about his illegitimate offspring in the lower city. Would she be open to hearing more truth about Yahweh, now that a few bricks around her heart had been removed?

"Do you remember only a few months before the siege began, when King Zedekiah ordered all Hebrew slaves released by their Hebrew owners?"

Her back straightened, but she didn't bristle. A conciliatory nod gave me permission to continue.

"Those slaves enjoyed only a few days' freedom before their Hebrew masters enslaved them again. That final act of rebellion, proving Judah's unyielding hardness of heart, was the reason Yahweh's discipline rained down on Jerusalem in our day."

Eyes wide, her face paled in the dim light of morning. "But how could I run my household without slaves? I couldn't do all the cooking and cleaning by myself."

I cradled her trembling hands in mine, amazed it didn't occur to her that she could have hired servants for a fair wage or joined them in the work. Rehearsing Helah's grousing over the smallest tasks, I realized how absurd my proposal would seem. "It's over now, Helah. Yahweh has disciplined His children, but His word through the prophets promises prosperity and blessing for our new lives in Babylon."

Shaking her head, she lingered in despair, but I captured her face gently between my hands. "You are my friend, Helah, and because Yahweh delivered Hebrews from bondage, I'll never call you my slave or treat you as such when we're alone. But when we're with the Scythians, you *must* obey me."

She searched my eyes, and finally, slowly, she nodded. "I will trust you, Merari. But I can't yet trust Yahweh."

CHAPTER 18

IDAN

"Johanan son of Kareah and all the army officers led away . . .
all those whom Nebuzaradan commander of the imperial guard had
left with Gedaliah . . .
the men, the women, the children and the king's daughters.
And they took Jeremiah the prophet and Baruch son of Neriah along
with them.
So they entered Egypt in disobedience to the LORD."
-Jeremiah 43:5–7

When Nebuchadnezzar received a messenger from General Nebuzaradan, we waited two nights in Aleppo for him to arrive, losing valuable time. The king insisted his harp player shelter at the same inn he chose for himself and his commanders. Merari shared a chamber with her handmaid, and Azat was chosen to sleep outside her door. He seemed too eager to spend more time with the Jewess. I was suddenly relieved I hadn't killed the old slave, who now seemed an immovable wall of protection around her mistress.

When the general finally arrived at dusk of our second day in Aleppo, a watchman cried, "The king's spoils approach!"

But the king's spoils were rotten. Over half the captives would die within two days and the temple's treasure had been chopped into small pieces, most items' original form unidentifiable.

Seething, Nebuchadnezzar called the general and his commanders together after dark. "You've ruined the Temple treasures." He swirled his goblet of wine as he spoke. "I hope you've brought good news about the prophet Jeremiah. Will he relocate to Babylon and pray for my prosperity and blessing?"

Nebuzaradan cleared his throat. "Jeremiah has been taken to Egypt, my king."

Nebuchadnezzar slammed his goblet on the table. "Taken?"

The general went to one knee, head bowed for the retelling. "Jews from every nation flocked to Jerusalem when they heard the siege had ended. The governor you appointed, Gedaliah, was assassinated by Jewish insurgents, who also killed several of my men. They escaped to Egypt before my men could track them and took hostages—Zedekiah's daughters, other wealthy Jews . . ." He cast uneasy glances at the commanders around the small circle. "The prophet Jeremiah and his scribe were among the hostages, my king."

"Will the prophet curse Babylon and bless Egypt?" Nebuchadnezzar's face flushed crimson, but his tone remained level.

"No, my king." The general's eyes brightened. "My spies say the exact opposite. The prophet tried to dissuade his captors from fleeing to Egypt, vowing Yahweh's curse unto death if they went and His blessing if they took him to Babylon. But they refused to listen."

Glaring at his general, Nebuchadnezzar spun his goblet

between two fingers. "Any spy who can hear that conversation and fail to rescue my prophet deserves death. Make it so, General, and have your men ready to march before dawn."

"But, my king, we just arrived from a week's march without . . ." Nebuzaradan's plea drowned in Nebuchadnezzar's unspoken threat. "Yes, my king. We'll be ready."

I delighted in my lieutenant's trumpet call barely a half-night later. We mustered our caravan to the day's beginning, and the general and his soldiers could barely drag themselves from their tents.

"Idan." Merari's hushed voice startled me from my stallion's hypnotic sway.

I looked over my shoulder.

"No, turn around. Turn around. I don't want Azat to know I'm talking to you."

"Then why are you talking? I have no secrets from my brother." That was a lie, but I didn't want her stirring more dangerous doubts.

"I'm afraid Azat may have feelings for me. You must talk to him. I'm going back to Babylon to find my husband."

Squeezing my eyes shut, I cursed my foolish friend. He'd warned me to avoid Tabiti's spell. What about Merari's power to charm? At the same time, I cheered a little for him. He'd always thought himself too short, too unworthy to please a wife, so he'd never let a woman capture his heart. *But why this woman, Azat?* If I ignored her, perhaps she'd stop talking.

"Idan!"

I groaned. "You are worse than a wrinkle on my saddle, woman. Give me a peaceful day, or I swear by Tabiti, I'll stuff your mouth with gold and tie your head to that sedan."

"You must talk with him. I don't want to hurt him. Please."

"All right!" I squeezed the camel's reins. Perhaps I could

relinquish them and escape her incessant chatter. But what if she cast her spell on others? A deep breath and controlled sigh focused my determination. Six days to the next city. Six days attached to this—

"What will you say to him?"

"Aaahhh!" I halted my stallion and faced her. "I'll say he is never to speak to you again. You poison us with lies about an impotent god who either can't or won't protect his people, and I'm tired of your incessant ranting about his love and power. From now on, I will escort you to play your silly harp for the king, and you will stay away from Azat. Is that clear?"

Tilting her head with a strange little smirk, she looked around us before speaking quietly. "Are you angry because you believe in Yahweh or because Azat is spending more time with me than you?"

Stunned by her battle savvy, my fury was disarmed by a beautiful woman in a stinking sedan. "Both," I admitted, turning my eyes on the road ahead. "Before I stepped across Jerusalem's broken gates, I knew who I was and what I wanted. I knew there were seven gods in the highest heavens." The caravan continued past us while I drew Merari's camel aside and kept my voice low. "I believe Yahweh is real. Though I can't accept everything you've said about him. But if you tell anyone, I'll kill you—no matter how Azat feels about you or what Nebuchadnezzar has threatened. Do you understand?"

"I understand very well, Prince Idan, and I'm saddened by your captivity."

Her comment hit me like an arrow to the heart, as I'm sure she intended. Ignoring her, I prodded my stallion and led both our mounts back into the caravan's flow. Merari remained silent the rest of the day, even when Azat attended to her needs at respites along the way.

We were all ready for our mats after a light meal at dusk, so I was less than pleased when I heard Azat's whisper in the growing gloom. "She won't talk to me now. What did you say to her today?"

I let out a sigh that could have felled an oak. "If you want her, Azat, take her. She sleeps on the other side of that curtain."

He slammed his hand over my mouth, and I bolted to my feet, dagger drawn. Azat stood opposite me, his blade at the ready. I lifted my empty hand. "Reflex, my friend. Reflex." We dropped our knives into the ground.

I didn't want to fight him, but something needed to change. Scrubbing my face, I stepped toward the tent flap. "We need to talk." He followed and we sat side by side on a fallen log, arms resting on our knees, as we'd done since we were boys. But this conversation was more difficult than most. "I know you have feelings for Merari, but she's going to Babylon to find her husband. You can't have her."

"Babylon has many provinces, Idan. What are the odds—"

"Only a few have a high population of Jews. Nebuchadnezzar tried to scatter them, but they regathered. They're a determined people." I faced him, not wishing to hurt him, but needing him to understand. "Merari has that same determination to find her husband, Azat. The connection of a husband and wife is hard to explain to someone who hasn't yet experienced it. Though you and I have spilled our blood into a cup and drunk the wine of brotherhood, we remain two individuals with separate lives and paths. But Zoya and I are one. Our lives are one, joined by our son. My arms ache for them and—"

"I understand the difference—"

"No, Azat. You don't. When I thought Merari was the goddess, I wanted her in my arms because she could return me to Zoya. Now, she's a woman stirring unwanted questions about her foreign god."

"When Merari was Tabiti, she held nothing I desired—no power, no promise, no purpose. Now, as a woman, she's everything I've longed for." He picked up a twig and began breaking it into pieces. "My heart will break if she finds her husband, but at least I'll know she's happy—and I will have known a beautiful woman of noble character."

CHAPTER 19

MERARI, REZEPH IN ASSYRIA

*"Indeed, to them you are nothing more than one who sings love songs
with a beautiful voice and plays an instrument well,
for they hear your words but do not put them into practice."*
-Ezekiel 33:32

*W*ater and food had been rationed for our six days of travel through the waterless forests between Aleppo and Rezeph, and on our sixth grueling day, I offered Helah the last drop of water from our shared skin.

"No, you take it." She shoved it away, her lips cracked and dry.

I pressed it to her lips and tipped it up, ignoring her protests. "Idan promised we'd reach Rezeph by dusk. You'll ride the rest of the way in the sedan with me." I spoke loud enough for the Scythian commander to hear. My friend's feet were blistered and swollen. She needed rest, and I prayed we'd stay at least a few days in Rezeph before the final, eighteen-day march along the Euphrates to Babylon's first city.

Without asking permission, I led Helah to the sedan and

began playing my harp. I'd started the practice on the first day out of Aleppo, with Idan's secret declaration of faith in Yahweh. My words seemed only an annoyance to him. Perhaps my harp could offer some solace to the captives—and captors —as they walked.

On the first day, I played every Psalm of David I could recall, singing in less-than-perfect pitch but with all my heart. The soldiers laughed and sang over me with bawdy war songs, mocking and rude. By the second day, however, even the roughest were silenced by David's praise. On day three, Idan joined with his mouth harp, and a few others—both captive and captor—unveiled instruments to play along. Soldiers from every nation tapped, blew, beat, and strummed praises to Yahweh, the God of heaven and earth. Tears streamed down my cheeks, a glorious grieving for Yahweh's people, silent and bitter among the praise of ignorant pagans.

We reached Rezeph at dusk as predicted, weary and worn. The king still demanded his harpist, and Azat again volunteered to escort me. Idan allowed it, though Helah was too exhausted to attend. I urged her to remain at the tent, prepare a meal, and sleep in case we broke camp early tomorrow.

Azat was chatty on the way to the king's tent since we'd spent little time together while traveling. "This King David you've spoken of, the harpist, he was a short man like me?"

"Short like us," I corrected, mocking my own stature. "Though the smallest of his brothers, he killed a giant with a sling and a single stone because he trusted Yahweh."

"No, Merari. He killed a giant with a slingshot, not his trust."

I grinned, accepting the challenge. "Without trust, Azat, he would never have confronted a giant with a slingshot."

Azat slowed as we approached the king's tent, gently

touching my arm to stop our progress. "Why is trust so important to your god? The Scythian gods don't care if I trust them. I trust only Idan's friendship and my courage. That's enough."

I looked into his sparkling, almond-shaped eyes, and placed a hand on his cheek. "People and courage may fail, but Yahweh is a Fortress whose mercies are new every morning."

He captured my palm and turned a gentle kiss into it.

I gasped at the fire racing up my arm and pulled away. *Yahweh, forgive me.*

"Merari, I—"

I rushed past him into the king's tent. He followed, thankfully, with my harp, removed its cover, and met my gaze, offering a tentative grin. A peace offering.

I resisted the urge to touch his cheek again.

"I want more singing!" Nebuchadnezzar roared from his throne, clapping. Servants scurried throughout the tent. His commanders sat in clusters on cushions scattered before the king. He held up a silver goblet and searched the tent. "More wine! I want more wi—My little harp maker. You kept me waiting. Play. Play right now!"

"Yes, my king." I bowed, hands trembling, and took a step toward the throne.

Azat grabbed my arm. "Don't get close," he whispered, watching the king. "He's drunk and agitated."

"Leave the harp player to her business." General Nebuzaradan appeared from the shadows and pulled me away from Azat. "The king will take good care of his pretty little Jewess tonight."

Azat struggled against two of the king's bodyguards. "Get your hands—" A blow to his middle doubled him over, and he was dragged outside.

The general pushed me to my knees at Nebuchadnezzar's feet. "Your harpist, my king."

"I thought I threw you out already." The king's lip curled, and he spit to his left side.

Backing away, the general stared at me like a cobra about to strike. The king touched my shoulder, and I jumped as if he'd shot me with an arrow.

"Play, Merari." His tone firm and quiet. "Now."

With trembling hands and a prayerful heart, I strummed the prayers of David, the song of Moses, the praises of Asaph—and tried with all my might to block out what might be happening to Azat outside the tent. *Please, Yahweh, protect my friend. Forgive my unexpected desire. And help me find Elon—before my heart betrays me.*

"Merari." Someone shook my shoulder, interrupting my songs. "Merari, come. I'll take you home."

I opened my eyes and realized I'd been strumming my harp in an exhausted stupor. "How late is it?"

"Very late." Arioch, the king's personal guard, offered a rare smile. Motioning me to follow, he led me around snoring commanders. I glimpsed the king splayed on his throne in drunken slumber just before exiting the tent into the starry night.

The cool night air slapped me with a memory. "Where's Azat?"

Arioch kept walking, his voice a coarse whisper. "I think the prince reached him in time to save him, but General Nebuzaradan is a dangerous enemy. You, too, must be careful, little Merari. The king's favor is the only thing protecting you."

Emotion tightened my throat, reality stirring both fear and sorrow. We drew near Idan's tent, where two clay lamps sputtered under the canopy, illuminating Helah tearing a robe into thin strips. *Bandages.*

I ran to her, leaving Arioch behind. Sobbing, I fell to my knees and into her arms. "Is Azat inside? Is he alive?"

"*Shh*, yes. He's—"

"He'll recover." Idan stood at the tent opening, arms crossed over a bare chest covered in blood. "No thanks to you."

Arioch stood over me. "It's your private war with the general that brought this on your captain, Prince Idan. Swallow your pride, and make peace with the general before you lose more good men." He nodded at me and left.

Idan stared after him for a dozen heartbeats. "Azat is asking for you." He ducked inside the tent before I could ask about his condition.

Hesitantly, I followed. A dozen lamps lit the space around a fresh reed mat. The man lying on it was unrecognizable. Both eyes swollen shut, his face was cut and bruised as were his arms and abdomen. Idan had covered him from the waist down with a light blanket and propped him against several pillows.

"Merari? Is it you?"

Idan turned his back to Azat and whispered his report. "Several ribs are broken, so I've got him propped up to breathe. We won't know about his vision until the swelling resolves. The same goes for the movement in his legs. For now, don't touch him."

I covered my mouth to stifle a sob and gain control. All the rage I'd felt for my sister came rushing back. The hate. The fury. Not the same loss of humanity when I found my son's body—no, that was another creature in me, more brutal than I could ever have conceived—but the thirst for vengeance rekindled.

Through clenched teeth, I ground out the words, "Kill. General. Nebuzaradan." Idan's shock was somehow satisfying.

"Merari?" Azat called for me again.

"Yes, it's me." I knelt, careful not to touch him, but when he gasped for air, I had to cradle his hand in mine. Kissing his bloodied knuckles, I let my tears fall. "I'm so sorry. I saw the general take you out. I should have told the king."

"The king saw them, Merari. He wouldn't have stopped this." He squeezed my hand. "I am sort of hoping you'll let me ride in that plush sedan of yours." He tried to smile, but I saw the cost in a cut that split open his top lip.

Everything in me yearned to stroke his cheek, tend his wounds, and care for this man who had been willing to give his life if the king defiled me.

"Letting me ride in the sedan doesn't make you unfaithful to your husband, Merari. I know you must search for him."

My silence had communicated rejection. "Of course, you'll ride in the sedan. That's not what I was think—"

He squeezed my hand again. "Please, listen. I won't stop you from looking for him, but promise me something . . ." He paused. "Is Idan here?"

"Yes, Azat. I'm here."

"If she doesn't find her husband, my friend, I plan to marry this Jewess. You'd better get used to the idea."

I heard a gasp and looked over my shoulder. Had the sound come from Scythia's crown prince or from me?

CHAPTER 20

IDAN

"The word of the LORD came to [Ezekiel]:
'Son of man, mark out two roads for the sword of the king of Babylon
to take,
both starting from the same country.
Make a signpost where the road branches off to the city.'"
-Ezekiel 21:18–19

J approached my tent as the sun glowed pink in the eastern sky. The old cow sat over the fire ring, striking flint stones. "King Nebuchadnezzar sent a messenger." She looked up, her brow creased with genuine concern. "You should hurry." Her words felt like boulders landing in my stomach.

I jogged toward the white tent in the center of camp and, while still a hundred paces away, saw General Nebuzaradan duck in before me. Rage stirred the boulders in my gut, and I was glad I hadn't eaten anything. I'd spent all night tending Azat's wounds, seething at his stubborn declaration to marry the Jewess, and I'd just left 3,100 angry Scythians in a clearing outside of town.

Yermek, Azat's first lieutenant, had arrived outside my tent when the sky glowed amethyst, just before dawn. He led me to a clearing beyond shouting distance, where all 3,100 Scythians had gathered—without my knowledge or command—to plan vengeance on the general and his regiment while they slept. "Valiant and brave," I shouted, "but how will you fight the rest of Nebuchadnezzar's army?" My warriors' feats of bravery and daring were legendary, but strategy eluded them. I needed all 3,100 alive to take my father's throne, but I also needed to retain their respect and loyalty. The rage I'd seen in Merari's eyes last night was multiplied by thousands in dawn's increasing light. I would lose my command if I couldn't deliver a measure of justice for my friend, their captain.

"When Azat recovers," I shouted, "we'll take our vengeance. If we were to attack now, the very man we seek to honor—lying vulnerable and unprotected on a mat in our camp—would be their first target." Begrudging nods allowed me to continue. "Trust me to lead you, Brothers, and we will return to Scythia as victors to build a nation where brotherhood and courage are the pillars on which we stand." A mighty war cry sent me on my way, and Yermek took charge of the troops, beginning drills with both axes and swords.

I paused a moment before entering Nebuchadnezzar's tent, gathering my wits. The general was laughing and chattering like a hoopoe about an Edomite soldier. Disgusted, I sighed and prepared for the coming battle.

The king noticed my arrival immediately. "Prince Idan, you're late."

"Apologies, my king. Since your general nearly killed my

captain last night, I had to place my lieutenant in charge of this morning's drills."

Nebuzaradan cast a condescending gaze down his long nose. "I object to the Scythian's accusation that—"

"Do you really want to lie to me?" The king leaned on the arm of his throne.

"No, I . . . Well, we didn't *nearly kill* him."

The king turned to me. "How will you exact your revenge, Scythian?"

"I'm open to suggestions, my king."

"I suggest you forget it happened. We leave Rezeph in two days as a *unified* army with a meager captive train and significant bounty from Yahweh's Temple." He leaned forward. "A personal vendetta among my commanders can only complicate the long journey back to Babylon."

"And a worthless leader can complicate a long journey."

"Worthless leader? You filthy—" The general swung at me.

I blocked the blow and shrugged off further attempts while four of his own guards restrained him. I spread my hands, showcasing the unruly general. "I'm concerned, my king, that all the troops will be damaged by such an undisciplined leader."

"Get your hands off me." Nebuzaradan groused and straightened his armor.

The king waved the guards away. "Leave us, General."

"What?" The general looked as if he'd been slapped. "I did nothing wrong, Neb. He's trying to poison—"

"Leave now!" Nebuchadnezzar stood, towering over us.

"Neb?" I asked. Who called the King of the World, *Neb*?

A hint of a grin relaxed the king into his throne as the general stormed out of the tent. "Nebuzaradan has been my friend since childhood. Our mothers are still friends. I'd never hear the end of it if I killed him."

I settled to one knee, relaxed but respectful. "Then you understand my difficulty. Azat is *my* childhood friend. He has no mother, no other family but me. We drank the cup of brotherhood, and I can't—I won't—let *anyone* hurt him."

"And I won't let a Scythian prince—or anyone else—kill Nebuzaradan." He groaned while massaging his temples.

"Too much wine last night?"

"Yes. So much I hardly remember hearing your little Jewess play her harp." His eyes brightened. "The Jewess!"

I shook my head, certain I'd hate any idea involving Merari.

"We'll divide the Jews, sending part with you and your Scythians in two days to begin the journey to Sippar. Nebuzaradan and I will wait here in Rezeph for an additional week with the remaining Jews and the bounty from the Temple."

It was ridiculous. "Why split the captives?"

"You'll travel more quickly without the wagons and with fewer captives on foot."

I stood before the greatest military mind in the world and could see no benefit for his troops in this plan. Why would he allow my men to strike out alone with the Jews? "My king, the Scythians have served you well with courage and might. Why not release us to go home now?" In a desperate effort, I added, "When I successfully assume my father's throne, I vow Scythia's lasting allegiance to Babylon in all military campaigns." It was a long-term commitment to future mercenary service, but well worth early release.

He studied me, and my mouth went dry. When he leaned forward, I felt like a rodent in the path of a viper. "Your Scythians will escort two thousand Jews to the three largest

Jewish-populated cities in Babylon. Then you may take your warriors home."

Not what I'd hoped, but it was better than placing all the Jews. We could return to Scythia in half the time if we weren't slowed by the whole caravan.

Merari's husband! The thought struck me like a blade. What if he wasn't in one of the three cities? Could Azat return to Scythia without her? Merari had never actually agreed to marry him, but she'd never agree until she was certain her husband was dead.

"I must be allowed to send messengers to inquire in every city where you've placed Jews."

A crease marred his forehead—and then understanding dawned. "You wish to find Merari's husband."

"I must."

He scrubbed his bearded chin. "The artisans and soldiers taken from Jerusalem eleven years ago were relocated to four cities. Three are governed by Jews I brought to Babylon when they were young boys; brothers named Shadrach, Meshach, and Abednego."

"And the fourth city?"

"The fourth is the capital. The city of Babylon cultivates the finest talent of every nation." He stood then, his final decision set in narrowed eyes. "You will place two thousand Jews in the three cities already thriving with their countrymen, but you will not step foot in my capital. After you've placed all your Jews, I'll send you enough gold and troops to help steal your father's throne."

It was the promise I'd been waiting for. What were the odds that Merari's husband was in the capital? "All right," I said, offering my hand in pledge. "Keep your general away from me and my men during the next two days, and we'll place your captives in three cities."

We locked wrists, securing a promise I could live with—but could my troops live without vengeance? Could Merari live with the uncertainty?

CHAPTER 21

MERARI

"When hope's dream seems to drag on and on, the delay can be depressing.
But when at last your dream comes true, life's sweetness will satisfy your soul."
-Proverbs 13:12

*I*dan returned sullen from his meeting with Nebuchadnezzar and in a hurry to leave our tent. He rummaged through his saddlebag. "Where is my wrist guard?"

"Shh!" I laid my hand across the harp strings to silence the song that had lulled Azat to sleep and pointed at his swollen eyes. "I demand to know how you'll repay the general."

"I don't answer to you, woman!" He stomped out.

Azat stirred. "Idan?"

I pressed his shoulder back against the pillows. "He's gone now, my friend. Sleep." I strummed again on my harp and hummed, hoping to calm myself as much as him. I heard Idan's low rumble outside but couldn't make out his words. I looked through the narrow slit as Helah scurried away at his command. She was my maid. Where was she going? Frustration welled up, and I clenched my teeth, strumming harder.

Azat's hand halted my playing. "You're agitated. I hear it."

I sighed, silently upbraiding myself. "Idan returned from his meeting with the king and won't tell me what was decided."

He brushed my hand. "I can tell you what was decided."

"Oh, really? Your injuries have improved your hearing?"

"I am the mighty little man, after all." A slight grin appeared between a patchy day's growth of stubble. "Idan decided to do what's best for Scythia."

I shoved his hand away. "You mean he decided to do what's best for Idan."

"He will be king, Merari. It's the same thing."

"How can you lie there in pain with blind trust?"

"That's what it means to be a soldier, Merari. I trust my commander. I obey without question. And I protect the brotherhood."

I scoffed at his steadfast words. "I've seen you argue and even fight Idan when you disagreed. How can you say you obey without question?"

He chuckled then. "I was afraid you'd pick that one out. I'm better at protecting Idan than trusting and obeying him, but now"—he tried to lift both arms, but his left hand barely moved—"I can only trust and obey."

The words struck me like a Scythian axe. *Trust and obey. Trust and obey.* Again and again, it rang in my head. "Rest now, Azat."

I rushed out of the tent, fell to my knees, and wept alone. Our camp was quiet, the men drilling with weapons and Helah on her errand for Idan. I was left to focus on the Commander of Heaven's Hosts. Could I trust and obey *Him* after so much loss? My son. My home. My life. And now . . . the near loss of an enemy who was stealing my affection.

Yahweh—the Great I Am. El-Roi—God who sees me. El-Shaddai —God Almighty. You, who knit me together in my ima's womb, come near so I can pour out before you all my broken pieces. Death surrounds me. Evil mocks me. Life eludes me. Joy has fled. Anger is my food; sorrow the wine at my feast. Fear has gone and dread replaced it; death an intriguing place on my map. A shortcut perhaps? A blade at my wrist could shorten my days. Would I see You or forever lick the flames of Sheol? The risk too great, the fear stirs rage, and I can't escape. Rescue me from the pit, O Lord. Only Your strong arm can reach so low. Only Your sharp eyes can see these depths. Only Your sweet heart can know my journey—and reach the end before me.

"Merari?" It was Helah's voice I heard. Not Yahweh's. Never Yahweh's. How many times in my life had I prayed, but He never answered? Did He speak only to prophets like Jeremiah? What good had it done my cousin? Bitterness rose like bile, drawing my knees up and my head down in a cocoon no one could enter.

Helah drew near, but I remained sequestered in my despair. She dropped something beside me, and warm, soft arms enfolded me. "Has something else happened? Is Azat . . ." She ran into the tent, and I heard her huff. Then she ranted at me for frightening her.

I couldn't answer. I was empty. Unable to move. I knew only that God had abandoned me. Hopelessness hid my face and sealed my lips, while Helah resumed her chores around me. By afternoon, I'd fallen on my side, eyes closed, and someone threw a blanket over my head. I woke after dark beside Helah in our tent chamber. Groaning, I turned over.

"Merari?" Helah raised on one elbow. "Love, are you all right?" Tears stung my eyes but no words came. I couldn't face her. Had she been right? Was Yahweh a legend of prophets to frighten the masses? She rubbed my back. "You'll feel better in the morning."

I woke to Idan's face hovering above me. "Are you finished with your tantrum?"

"Get out of there! Leave her alone." Helah flew at him with a dishcloth, waving it like a battle axe.

I rolled over and closed my eyes again, but Helah sat at my back and hung her head over my shoulder. "You must eat something, my girl. I can't care for a half-dead soldier and you too. I need help. We leave in two days." She shoved a piece of bread in my hand. "Eat!"

Helah won no awards for compassion, but within two days, she'd managed to prepare for our eighteen-day journey to Sippar, Babylon's first city. Filling and stacking baskets, using her new mortar and pestle to crush dried herbs, and purchasing enough grain and wine to sustain our tent-family of four, Helah stayed busy while I held Azat's hand.

Idan spent two days preparing his regiment for the journey but gave no inkling to the captives about our destinations. On the morning of our departure, he fought his first unexpected battle.

Helah kept her voice low but mirrored Idan's posture, fists at her waist and feet apart. "How do I care for Merari and Azat if I walk on the ground and they're on the camel? They both need me, and there's plenty of room for all three of us in that sedan with the new pillows you bought." Without waiting for his approval, she stepped around him and joined Azat and me in Mara's sedan. It was the first time I'd smiled in three days.

Placing my harp in my arms, she nodded toward the soldiers falling into ranks behind us. "Play something soothing. Our lives may depend on it."

Startled by the cryptic comment, I shaded my eyes and saw General Nebuzaradan approaching the three thousand tattooed Scythians with at least five hundred men on horseback. Idan's warriors drew their battle axes, while the Jewish captives huddled in protective clusters. Idan prodded his stallion, placing himself between the Babylonians and his men. "Stand down! Stand down, all of you!" Turning to the general's horsemen, he shouted, "Ride away, or we fight!"

Nebuzaradan raised his fist in the air, halting his horsemen's advance. Grumbling and cursing Scythians drowned out more shouting, and Azat clutched at the cushions beside him. "Tell me what's happening! I see black, only black." His eyes, partially opened but still unseeing, were his greatest enemy now.

I slid onto the cushions beside him and breathed softly against his cheek. "Nothing's happening, my friend. Idan is masterful. He's safe, and he has diffused the situation." I eyed Helah, who waited with an infusion of poppy tea. "You must stay calm, or Helah will make you sleep through our departure." Any thrashing opened the knife wounds on his sides, arms, and legs.

Reaching for my hand, he gripped it with surprising strength. "Tell me everything you see, Merari. As if I were standing beside Idan."

Fighting tears, I forced melancholy from my voice. "One day you'll stand beside him again, Azat." Helah's brows dipped, but I warned her with a stare. Now wasn't the time to tell Azat our concerns about his useless leg or sightless eyes.

"Idan has regained control, and Nebuzaradan is leading away his troops." He knew I was lying. Both sides continued shouting threats. I saw only Idan's back, and Azat didn't need a description of Nebuzaradan's smirk.

"Look in the opposite direction, Merari," Azat whispered.

"I'm all right, Azat. I don't need your coddling. I—"

"Look in the opposite direction, now!"

"What do you mean *the opposite direction?*" I rose to my knees in the sedan, searching the northeastern horizon, and saw a single horseman dressed in a wool robe.

Azat's hand brushed my arm, his sudden tenderness matching his now gentle voice. "Is there a Babylonian soldier speeding out of camp—unnoticed?"

I swallowed hard. "It's a single rider in a rough-spun robe, but yes. What does it mean?"

"Sit." He patted the cushion beside him.

"If I sit, I can't see over the sedan. How will we know if Idan is safe?" Or if he was sweetening his position for Scythia's throne? He'd done nothing but appease the Babylonians for two days.

"Please, Merari," Azat said, settling back into the cushions. "Play your harp louder than the noise."

"But I—"

"Sit down, Merari, and play." It wasn't a request.

"You must be feeling better. You're getting bossy." He smiled, but I wasn't kidding. How did a man who could barely move command me? But I obeyed and began strumming my harp, while Helah wiped Azat's brow with a trembling hand. The shouting outside our cushioned world faded as Mara started her slow and steady pace. We traveled without stopping until midday, and my fingers continued to dance over the strings, numb by the time we reached our first respite.

Tapping Mara's hind quarters, I planned to dismount and stretch my legs but recoiled at Idan's outstretched hand. "I thought you said Nebuchadnezzar would keep his general away from you and Azat."

He grabbed my arm, pulling me away from other ears. "General Nebuzaradan's appearance at our departure was a diversion. My spies say a messenger on horseback left the camp, headed northeast." He shoved me away. "Yermek!"

The baby-faced lieutenant bounded over. "Yes, Commander?"

"You will guard your captain and the women in the sedan during our respites. Escort them wherever they go. Understood?"

"Yes, sir." He pounded his fist against his chest and extended his other hand toward a copse of trees—as if I would relieve myself in front of a strange man.

"Never mind." I would hold it until we reached Babylon if needed.

I started to climb back into the sedan, and heard Idan chuckle. "It's going to be a long eighteen days." Ignoring him, I returned to my perch, trying to block out the vile jokes of Scythian soldiers. Helah climbed down, anxious to find a private place in the trees.

Azat grasped the new headscarf Helah had purchased for me between two fingers, enjoying its silky softness. "Blue looks good on you."

I covered a gasp. "You can see!" I shouted over the sedan wall. "Idan, Azat can see!" I nearly hugged him, but caught myself, awkwardly patting his arm instead.

He captured my hand and turned it over, kissing my palm.

"Someday I'll enjoy your embrace. For now, I'm simply happy to see you again."

Warmth traveled up my arm and into my heart. His sight was an unexpected gift. Perhaps Yahweh hadn't abandoned me completely. *Thank You, Lord God of all Creation. If You are there, open my eyes to see You as You've opened Azat's to see me.*

CHAPTER 22

IDAN, WILDERNESS ON THE EUPHRATES RIVER

*"I will make them abhorrent and an offense to all the kingdoms of
the earth,
a reproach and a byword, a curse and an object of ridicule, wherever
I banish them."*
-Jeremiah 24:9

I stood on the banks of the Euphrates, casting a long shadow over still waters. My regiment made camp for the sixteenth night of our eighteen-day journey. I still hadn't told anyone we were only placing captives in three cities. I'd kept the plan vague during the two-day preparation in Rezeph, giving only the name of our first destination—Sippar—a city governed by Meshach, one of the Jewish men the king mentioned.

A twig snapped behind me, and I whirled, ready to fight. Azat slid down the slippery riverbank, his crutch flying into the air. I dropped my dagger and caught him before he tumbled into the Euphrates. He was laughing hysterically by the time my heart started beating again.

I wanted to be angry, but . . . "You are insane!" Shoving him to the ground, I plopped down and laughed beside him.

"You'd be insane, too, if you had to ride in a camel's sedan with two women for two weeks." He was right, of course, and the comment sent us into more hysterics.

Two weeks' travel on high alert had driven all of us to the edge of sanity. I'd sent two spies to follow Nebuzaradan's secret messenger, but neither had returned to report. Now, only four days until we reached Sippar, I needed to accept that my spies were either traitors or dead. Not only was Nebuchadnezzar the most brilliant military mind in the world, but his general—a man with no honor—had also proven my superior.

My laughter wound down as reality weighed heavily. I had led my troops into an uninhabited wilderness with two thousand captives, dwindling supplies, and a wounded best friend who was becoming too enthralled with a foreign god.

"We're almost there, Idan." Azat grasped my shoulder and shook it. "Our men are well trained and capable. We'll meet any obstacle that comes." His encouragement felt forced and patronizing.

I ignored him, listening instead to the captives' songs that had been a constant balm, day and night. Harps and lyres, timbrels and drums. My soldiers' mouth harps added a Scythian twang to the unique Zion songs, and I closed my eyes, enjoying what had been my only salvation on this journey. It soothed and calmed—but so much more. Within three days of leaving Rezeph, those suffering from plague symptoms—both captives and soldiers—began showing dramatic improvements. The kind of improvements that should have taken weeks.

I glanced at Azat as he leaned back on strong arms and marveled again at his recovery. Eyesight completely restored, his only lingering impairment was a right foot that dragged behind him. I didn't dare think on it too long.

Reaching into my waist pouch, I retrieved my mouth harp and placed it between my front teeth. Breathing in and out, I gently tapped my finger against the reed, making the familiar sounds I'd played since my uncle taught me as a boy. I remembered happier times with Uncle Anach, an intellectual more skilled with mind than sword. Never married, he loved me like his own, and because Father was jealous of our kinship, he sent him to distant lands to expand Scythia's culture. When Anach returned with an affinity for Greek gods, my father wanted him dead—by my hand.

"Aaahhh!" Peace destroyed, I threw my harp into the river, sniffing back emotion as if still holding the bloody knife.

"How can I help you, Idan?" Azat spoke quietly, calmly. When had he become the rational one?

I let the river sounds massage my heart. "Did I ever tell you Uncle Anach's story about how the first lyre was made?"

"Tell me."

"It was made by the Greek god Hermes, who stole a cow from his brother Apollo. Hermes slaughtered the cow, cleaned and dried the entrails, and then stretched them as strings over a hollowed-out piece of wood to make lovely sounds that would engender Apollo's forgiveness."

"Do you believe the story?"

"That's a dangerous question to ask a Scythian, Azat." I met my friend's gaze and held it. "Anach told me that story right before I slit his throat." Lying back on the grassy bank, I laced my hands behind my head and addressed the real issue between us. "It doesn't matter that a flock of birds chased away hyenas in Hamath or that captives have been healed of plague in a few days, Azat. We're Scythians. We don't believe in

Yahweh. Even if I believed personally, I couldn't bring such a radical change to our people after taking my father's throne. Our people would rebel and our nation spiral out of control."

He leaned over me, searching my eyes. "Tell me all of it. What else is bothering you?"

I could delay the news no longer. "Nebuchadnezzar gave permission to disperse the Jews in only three cities."

Betrayal flashed in his eyes, but he tamped it down—like a good soldier. "What if we don't find Merari's husband in any of the three—"

I sat up, ready for battle. "You're *my* captain, not *her* keeper!"

He inclined his head in calm submission. "You're my king and my brother, Idan. My loyalty is to you first and always."

His devotion pierced me, exposing my pettiness. "We'll send messengers to every city with a Jewish population to inquire about Merari's husband, Azat. If he's alive, we'll find him."

He grabbed his crutch and stood without looking at me. "I need to tell you something I saw in a dream."

"A dream?" I laughed, thinking he was kidding. "What are you now, a prophet?"

But he met my gaze, and I saw no mirth. "Nebuchadnezzar will betray you, Idan. I've seen it."

"You've seen . . . What? How do you know? Wait." I clenched my teeth. "If it has anything to do with Yahweh, don't tell me."

After another long silence, he climbed the riverbank and left me wondering why Yahweh spoke to a Scythian in his dreams.

CHAPTER 23

MERARI, SIPPAR IN BABYLON

"Along the banks of Babylon's rivers we sat as exiles, mourning our captivity,
and wept with great love for Zion.
Our music and mirth were no longer heard, only sadness.
We hung up our harps on the willow trees."
-Psalm 137:1–2

The morning after Azat mentioned his dream to Idan, the commander woke before dawn and ordered our whole processional to begin its travel day immediately. He seemed driven by an unseen enemy, refusing to stop for our first respite until nearly midday.

Even then, he shouted at his lieutenants, "No napping under the shade trees! Eat, drink, and get back on the road." He tapped Mara's hind quarters, and gave Azat a sardonic grin. "Will you ever rejoin your regiment, or do you plan to ride with women for the rest of your days?"

I saw the hurt on Azat's expression, and felt the prickly

sting of anger in my cheeks. "How dare you? Azat still can't bear weight on his right foot. How could he mount a horse?"

"Be silent, woman!" Azat shouted.

Stunned and hurt, I handed him the crutch as he climbed from the sedan.

A smile lit Idan's face. "Bring the captain's stallion!"

When Azat took the crutch, he brushed my fingers, his expression tender and apologetic. By the time he turned around, every man in his hundred-man regiment had lined up on their mounts, saluting as he walked to take his horse's reins. With each step, I saw his strength return, his chest swell, his shoulders rise. He passed off the crutch to Yermek and held his stallion's head, pressing his face against the beast's nose and whispering to it like a lost love. Then, as if he'd never been injured, Azat sprang from one foot onto its back before I could even fear for his safety.

His whole countenance lit, and he released a war cry. The whole regiment joined him in ear-splitting bass tones, vibrating my chest. I waited for Azat to look at me, but he'd disappeared into the brotherhood of warriors, lost in the world of men I neither liked nor understood. He prodded his horse into a celebratory lap around the processional and took his customary position as rear guard. Idan cast a victorious glance at me, and I shivered.

Helah patted my hand but I pulled away. I was being ridiculous. Why should I need comfort? I was a married woman. How long had it been since I'd thought of Elon? We'd be searching for him in Babylon soon. How could I tell him about Neriah? The thought pierced me. *Yahweh, give me words.* I dropped my head, ashamed of my traitorous heart. Azat was a friend, nothing more. His marriage declaration was the impulsive reaction of a wounded warrior, and my emotions were as tumultuous as a summer storm. Even if the unthinkable happened, and I never found Elon, Azat was a Scythian, and I was a part of God's chosen people. The Law commanded that I remain pure in love and marriage to another of Israel's chosen.

Reaching for my harp, I ran my fingers over Elon's signature, struggling after eleven years to remember his face. Plucking the strings, I returned to the one thing I did remember. The songs of Zion. Always the songs of Zion. In them I could lose myself and remember home. In them I could find the Giver of Music.

After our midday respite, I returned to my wood-and-string friend who waited for me in the sedan. Our caravan began its march again, and step by step the music rose again, joining captive and captor in this final day of our journey to Babylon.

Shortly after the respite, Idan turned to face his troops and lifted two fingers to his mouth, releasing the loudest whistle I'd ever heard. "Sippar on the horizon!" he shouted. "Sippar on the horizon!"

I rose to my knees in the sedan, willing my eyes to see it, but his warrior's eyes were sharper than mine.

When I returned to the cushion, Helah reached for my hand. "What awaits us there, Merari? It's easier to die than to live in the unknown." Her lips trembled, and I saw more fear in her eyes today than when she faced King Nebuchadnezzar in Riblah.

She turned away before I could offer comfort, but what comfort had I to give? My fingers refused to play. Not a single harp or lyre was heard. The Scythians marched in silence toward the gates of Sippar where their captives would be dispersed, sold, and separated forever. By the time the sun fell to midafternoon, mud brick buildings and a tall, angular tower had come into view.

Curiosity conquered fear, and I climbed to my knees to ask Idan, "What's that tall structure?"

"It's a ziggurat, a temple where they worship Marduk, Nebuchadnezzar's patron god."

Ziggurat. Marduk. The unfamiliar terms knocked me back onto the cushions. I clutched my harp, so familiar and beloved in my world. Would there be anything familiar in Babylon? *I will forever be a stranger in a distant land.* What clothes would I wear? What foods would I eat? Strange varieties of trees lined the road, and farmers harvested a plant with small pods I didn't recognize.

I would never again see Judah. The crushing reality felt like a millstone around my neck. Could Yahweh dwell outside Jerusalem? I'd seen Him heal captives of plague while on our march and touch Azat's body miraculously, but did He dwell among pagans? *Yahweh, are You here?*

Our Scythian captors began celebrating as we drew nearer the city, but my countrymen appeared to shrink inside their skin. I saw my fears in their gaping mouths and ricocheting eyes. Idan raised his fist, calling the procession to a halt. The sound of galloping hooves approached, and I stifled a cry, hiding amid the cushions with Helah. A wave of relief washed over me when I saw Azat and the men of Idan's hundred-man regiment skid to a halt beside us. Mara buckled her legs for our dismount, but Helah reached for my hand. Neither of us were in a hurry to leave the sedan. I peeked over the sides and found the other captives had collapsed on the ground, cautious and wide-eyed like Helah and me.

Idan gestured wildly as he spoke, seeming revived and excited. "Have the men set up camp outside the city, supply wagons and exiles in the center. Assign three detachments to purchase supplies in Sippar's market. The citizens may begrudge us adding to their population, but the merchants will be pleased to take our gold and silver." He nodded to the captives in frightened huddles. "Take them to the river for baths. Perhaps the people of Sippar will accept them more willingly if they're clean." He turned to Azat. "Captain, you and Yermek will come with me to meet Sippar's governor—a Jew named Meshach."

"A Jew is *governor*?" I blurted my astonishment from Mara's sedan.

Idan's stare could have frozen the Euphrates. He returned his attention to his men. "You have your assignments. Sippar is the first of our three cities, so let's get our supplies, dispense of a third of the exiles, and be on our way to the second city. You're dismissed."

"Three cities?" I said, the implications slowly registering. "Three cities," I said again as Idan rode away. Panic rose as did my voice, and I screamed—on the verge of hysteria. "Azat, what did he mean by three cities?"

The man I thought my friend cast a glance over his shoulder and followed his commander without a word. I stared after them, disbelieving. Could I have been so blind? So foolish? Falling back on the cushions, I could barely breathe.

Helah's face was ashen. "Merari. My girl. I'm so sorry."

Idan's regiment hurried to their assigned tasks and mobilized the rest of the troops. A Scythian I'd never seen before approached Mara. "Get off the camel." He grabbed Helah's arm and dragged her from the sedan.

I flew at him, trying to rescue my friend, but the mountainous soldier grabbed my wrist and dragged me along with her. "Listen, little harp player, King Nebuchadnezzar said you were deity only until we arrived in Babylon."

I stumbled in the soft, black soil, and wondered how it had turned men's hearts to stone. Why had our peaceful captors suddenly reverted to the monstrous conquerors they'd been in Jerusalem and Riblah?

"Where are your songs of Zion now?" one of the soldiers shouted as my people bathed, fully clothed, in the muddy river.

One man hung his harp in a willow tree, but a soldier snatched it off and threw it into the river near him. "Play your harp, old man. Maybe the Babylonians in Sippar will let you live a day longer."

Their mocking stung worse than whips, making the harmony we'd experienced on our journey as torturous as the famine, plague, and sword in Jerusalem. How could we have so easily appeased our enemy, when it was the nature of compromise that had carried us into exile?

O Lord, may I never strum a harp again unless it is to praise You and honor Zion, the city I once called home.

CHAPTER 24

IDAN

*"The king appointed Shadrach, Meshach and Abednego
administrators
over the province of Babylon . . . [after their miraculous salvation
from the fiery furnace]*
The king promoted Shadrach, Meshach and Abednego in the province
of Babylon."
-Daniel 2:49; 3:30

*J*rode between Azat and Yermek toward Sippar's city
gate, where a man wearing a knee-length, gold-
belted robe waited. He raised his right hand in greeting,
holding the hem of a patterned cloak draped over his left arm.
A thick, hooked nose betrayed his Jewish birth, but the curled
and oiled beard proclaimed him thoroughly Babylonian in
culture. His position at the city gate boldly declared Scythians
weren't welcome in his city.

"Greetings, Commander Idan." Walking toward us, he
extended his free hand. "I'm Meshach, Governor of Sippar."

I reined my stallion to a halt, ignoring his hand. "How do you know my name, Governor?"

"The king sent a messenger with word of your imminent arrival." He took three more steps and grasped my stallion's bridle. With eyes communicating discretion, he hid a piece of parchment under a leather strap and whispered, "I'm saving your life."

He stepped back and assessed Azat and Yermek as if purchasing sheep at the market. "Your troops are more *enthusiastic* than our businesses are comfortable entertaining. Sippar is the gateway to Babylon, the trading center where the great river splits into five branches. As governor, I must ensure peace inside my walls, which means keeping any threat of chaos outside." He peered around me, nodding at the mayhem of shrieking captives and shouting Scythians behind us. "After the long trek across the wilderness, many caravans arrive at Sippar with a surge of energy that is best spent outside our gates. We will provide a loaf of bread for everyone in your procession, Commander, but only small contingents will pass through the gates to purchase supplies."

I held his gaze, unsure if I faced a friend or foe. "Your king trusts us, but you don't, Governor?"

"It is not my intention to offend, Prince Idan. In fact, I would be honored to have you and your officers join me for a meal this evening in my home. My guards will meet you at the gates by sunset and escort you. We'll enjoy some Babylonian cuisine and plan the exiles' placement in Sippar's businesses, households, and temples." He offered curt nods and turned to go.

"What about—"

"I'll answer all your questions this evening." He waved as he walked away, shouting over his shoulder.

"Should we be honored or insulted?" Azat asked, watching the man disappear into the city's busy market.

"Insulted," Yermek growled.

I leaned over to stroke my stallion's neck, lifting the parchment from its hiding place and tucking it under my belt. "We have plenty to do in camp before sunset. Yermek, you ride ahead of Azat and me. Take ten men from our regiment into town to scout the location of the governor's home. Azat and I will attend the governor's meal tonight, but I want our men ready if he's planned treachery."

The lieutenant saluted and prodded his stallion into a gallop back to camp. I withdrew the parchment from my belt and held it up. "Governor Meshach is skilled in secrets." After unfolding it, I read aloud, "King Nebuchadnezzar in league with your father."

"My dream fulfilled." Azat breathed the words, his face gray.

His dream from Yahweh. It felt like another betrayal. "Tell me the dream."

He drew both hands down his face with a weary sigh and closed his eyes as if watching it again in his mind. "King Nebuchadnezzar slipped into a tent where your father slept and poured honey in his ear. When your father woke, he emerged from the tent and gave Nebuchadnezzar seven fine stallions, the same man seated on each horse." Turning to me, he shook his head, sorrow leaking into his voice. "It was you, Idan. One of you on *seven* horses—the number of completeness. Your father gave you over to the King of the World."

The ball of hate grew in my belly, churning. "So I am not to be king of Scythia."

"If Governor Meshach gave you this message, perhaps he has more information."

I folded the parchment and returned it to my belt, focusing on the man I'd trusted all my life. "Do you serve me, Azat, or has Yahweh stolen your allegiance?"

His pained expression stalled my breathing, but he slammed his fist against his chest. "I will never fail you, my friend."

He didn't answer my question, but I still saw loyalty in his eyes.

CHAPTER 25

MERARI

"You can trust a friend who wounds you with his honesty, but your enemy's pretended flattery comes from insincerity."
-Proverbs 27:6

The ruffian soldier returned Helah and me from our baths to where Mara still lounged on the grass. Still soaking wet, my long, black hair hung loose down my back, my red robe clinging to my healthier frame.

Idan and Azat had returned from their meeting with the governor and hammered tent pegs into the ground as if driving them into stone. Idan noticed our arrival with a glance but ignored the soldier who escorted us.

The man cleared his throat to get Azat's attention. "They're clean but still stink of captivity." The captain looked up, his eyes taking inventory of my form.

Heat singed my cheeks. Was it anger or humiliation? I rushed to our donkey that carried food supplies, intent on setting up camp. Helah followed, silent.

Azat dismissed the vile soldier, and I breathed a sigh of

relief. At least Helah and I could prepare tonight's meal without fear for our lives. Or should we fear Idan and Azat now that we were in Babylon? I untethered the basket containing the hand mill, the last sack of grain, and our flint stones. I slung it over my shoulder and turned toward the tent, running headlong into Azat.

He captured me in his arms. "Let me explain." His whisper came from less than a handbreadth away.

"No!" I shoved him away. "Leave me alone." Fighting panic, I searched for a shady spot to escape him.

"Please!" He reached for my arm, pulling me around to face him.

"I'm going to catch some fish," Helah shouted from beside the donkey, lifting a rough-woven net in the air. "Would anyone like to come?"

"Go, Helah." Azat spoke calmly to her but stayed focused on me. "I just want to talk with her."

When my friend hesitated, Idan abandoned his tent project and walked toward her. "Go." With a mournful glance, she left me with my betrayers.

Idan threw down his hammer and reached for a waterskin. "Let's take her over there, Azat." He led the way to a shady spot beneath a willow tree, secluded from the rest of the camp.

Azat's hand was gentle on my arm, but I couldn't stop trembling. Everything had changed in Sippar. What would they do to me now? Anger gave way to terror, and my legs turned to water. Stumbling, Azat bent to catch me, and the kindness in his eyes cut me deeper than a dagger. I pulled my hand away. "Don't touch me." The words came out on a sob, and I followed Idan to the shade without Azat's hand to guide me.

The prince pointed to a fallen log where I was to sit. I obeyed. Azat stood beside him but said nothing. Idan removed a piece of parchment from his belt, unfolded it, and held it before me. "Read it."

King Nebuchadnezzar in league with your father. Was I supposed to care?

Azat sighed. "The governor secretly gave this message to Idan to help us."

Idan sat down opposite me. "Yahweh told Azat the same thing in a dream."

"Really?" Sarcasm dripped like honey. "Yahweh would never speak to a Scythian." Then I glared at Azat. "It sickens me to admit Yahweh spoke to a liar."

His spine stiffened. "I've never lied to you, Merari."

"You didn't tell me we were only going to three cities."

Idan threw the parchment at me. "And you forget yourself, woman. You are a captive of Babylon. We owe you nothing."

The truth stole my breath. He was right. I had nothing. No family. No possessions. No home. I stood, trying to escape before tears humiliated me. "Leave me alone then."

But Azat's gentle hand circled my waist, his lips pressed against my ear. "I have never lied to you, Merari. Please. Listen to Idan."

I covered a sob, infuriated by my weakness, and stood like a stone.

"Nebuchadnezzar commanded me to place exiles in the three cities with the largest Jewish populations. If your husband was as talented as you say, and he survived the exile, he's likely in the capital or one of these three cities."

I turned around to face Idan. "The capital?"

"Nebuchadnezzar forbade me to enter the city of Babylon, but I'll send messengers to every city in the province with known Jewish artisans—including the capital—to inquire about Elon."

He seemed sincere, and when I looked again at Azat, he lifted my hand and kissed my palm. "Idan will keep his word. He is a man of integrity."

I pulled my hand away, feeling more *married* in Sippar and still uncertain of Azat's intentions.

"Merari." My name on Idan's lips startled me, and the defeat I saw on his features was equally surprising. "I'll never be king of Scythia, but I still hold out hope to return, beg my father's forgiveness, and see my wife and son again."

The thought of anyone being separated from family pained me. "Surely, your father won't keep them from you."

The hard lines returned to his features. "My father has never cared about family. I can only hope that my three thousand loyal soldiers will be enough incentive to welcome me home." He motioned to Azat. "My captain will lead the men home if their loyalty turns toward my father. We'll know more after the meeting with Sippar's governor tonight."

Azat nodded and cast an unsure glance at me. My traitorous heart skipped a beat, and I blurted, "Would you like me to accompany you and play my harp for the governor?"

What did I just say?

Idan's eyes brightened. "That's a good idea. I'm sure Meshach would enjoy songs from his homeland."

I wanted to decline, make an excuse, reconsider, but the approval in Azat's eyes made it impossible. Hadn't I vowed to never again play the harp unless it was to praise Yahweh or honor Jerusalem? "I will play the songs of Zion then."

Idan's eyes met mine with a warmth I hadn't seen since he thought I was Tabiti. "I would expect nothing less."

CHAPTER 26

IDAN

"Son of man, mark out two roads for the sword of the king of Babylon to take, both starting from the same country. Make a signpost where the road branches off to the city."
-Ezekiel 21:19

I finished braiding my stallion's mane and pressed a kiss against his jaw. "You are my champion."

Azat finished primping his mount, and Merari emerged from the tent in a deep purple robe we'd found in one of the plunder wagons. She was dazzling. Azat couldn't take his eyes off her.

I thought of the harp wrapped in the blanket on my supply donkey. If I returned it tonight, would she praise me for saving it or hate me for keeping it from her all these weeks? I left it hidden and cleared my throat, realizing I'd been staring.

Azat leapt onto his horse with one good leg, and I hoisted Merari up behind him. Stiff at first, she awkwardly placed her hands on his shoulders. "Grab his waist or you'll kiss the ground when we gallop." I took two steps and swung onto my mount, and he started a gallop without a command. I looked over my shoulder halfway to the city and saw the Jewess, arms tight around Azat, laughing. She was good for him. They were good together.

As promised, a guard at the gate led us to Meshach's home, a two-story mud brick structure near the city's main entrance. A young girl with long brown hair welcomed us at his door, greeting Merari in Hebrew. We followed her through a lush courtyard of fruit trees and flowering bushes. After passing a tiered fountain, we arrived in the dining room, where Meshach waited at a low-lying table, already sipping a glass of wine.

"I see you brought friends, Prince Idan." He motioned to several cushions around the table. "Please, sit down."

We bowed, and I made introductions as we approached the table. "My captain and lifelong friend, Azat, and this is Merari. She lived in Jerusalem and played her harp while we were in King Nebuchadnezzar's camp."

Meshach studied her. "Merari, did you say?" He was on his feet, speaking in Hebrew before I could answer. "Did you realize your name matches the musical division of Levitical Temple servants?" He pointed to the harp Nebuchadnezzar had given her, tucked under her arm. "To be a woman with such talent is extraordinary."

"Thank you, my lord." Her voice quaked. "My husband was a Merarite and always said my name was the reason he chose me." Meshach laughed, and Merari's shoulders relaxed. She ducked her head and added, "Elon taught me to play. He was the finest harp maker in Jerusalem."

Meshach's smile dimmed. "Was?"

"He was taken in the exile eleven years ago." She lifted her eyes to meet his gaze. "I'm hopeful Yahweh will reunite us somehow, now that I'm a captive too. Do you know of Elon, Jerusalem's harp maker?"

Eyes kind, the governor shook his head. "I'm sorry, my dear, no. I know everyone in Sippar, and there is no harp maker, but if your Elon was Jerusalem's best, he would have likely been taken to Nippur or Erech, the cities my brothers govern." Looking to me, his expression was more command than request. "Commander, you'll need to ask Shadrach and Abednego specifically about Elon. They'll know if he's in their cities."

"Yes, my lord."

"Good. Good. Please, sit. Eat." He clapped his hands, and servants flooded the room, carrying roast meats, fresh fruits and vegetables, bread and cheeses. Merari took her place in the corner, preparing to play. "Oh, no," he said, waving her back to the table. "You're my guest. First, you eat. Then you play." He winked. "I'll want to hear the songs of Zion." Meshach dictated our places. Me, at his right. Azat, on his left. And Merari beside Azat. I wanted to dislike him or chafe at his authority or regard him with suspicion.

But he was entirely too likable.

He began a polite discussion about our journey from Rezeph, but I could wait no longer. "I need to know about the parchment."

"Yes, I'm sure you have many questions." He clapped his hands again, and another servant brought in a large scroll, positioning it on the table so we could all see it. "I received this from Yahweh's prophet almost seven years ago. Read that portion there, Prince Idan." He pointed with a lamb bone in his hand.

"I'm sorry, Lord Meshach. I speak Hebrew, but I don't read it. Would you mind reading it for me?"

"Of course. Of course. It says, '*Son of man*.'" He licked his fingers. "That's what Yahweh calls Ezekiel when He speaks a prophetic message to him. *"Son of man, mark out two roads for the sword of the king of Babylon to take, both starting from the same country."*

He looked up at me as if I was supposed to understand. "I'm sorry, Lord Meshach. Am I supposed to—"

"Seven years ago, Yahweh told Ezekiel that Nebuchadnezzar would divide his 'sword'—his army—and send the captives in two quantities from the same location. Like he did with you and General Nebuzaradan when he sent you from Rezeph. I knew it was Ezekiel's prophecy coming to pass when the general's spy arrived two days ago."

The hair on the back of my neck stood on end. Which was more disturbing—that the spy had come to this man with the general's message or the spiritual implications? "Why did the spy come to you?" I was more equipped for military strategy.

"I am to stall your departure. The king has given Nebuzaradan's assassins permission to kill you."

I reached for my wine goblet, willing my hand to remain steady. "My men won't let that happen."

Meshach took a slow sip from his goblet and set it back on the table. "If I were you, Prince Idan, I'd trust Yahweh's protection over your troops. If Yahweh knew seven years ago that Nebuchadnezzar would split both his troops and his captives, I'd wager He has a plan for you."

I set aside my wine, and shoved away the scroll. "That's all coincidence."

"Really?" Meshach's grin widened. "Is it a coincidence you've been ordered to deliver exiles to the only three cities in Babylon *governed* by Jews, and the remaining two governors are my brothers? Is it a coincidence that my brothers and I each have a personal knowledge of Yahweh's miraculous power to save?" He leaned close, eyes narrowing in challenge. "You're going to need that power to survive Babylon's treachery, my friend."

"Three brothers?" Merari interrupted. "You're not . . . Are you? King Nebuchadnezzar told me a story about three brothers saved from a smelting furnace . . ."

"Yes, my brothers and I refused to bend the knee to Nebuchadnezzar's ridiculous statue. It's still standing on the Dura Plain. You'll see it when you sail downriver to Nippur."

"What was He like?" Azat sounded breathless. "Yahweh, I mean."

"We don't have time for this." I slammed my hand on the table. "If Nebuchadnezzar wants me dead, I must leave the captives, take my men, and flee."

Meshach shook his head while I spoke. "You can't flee. You must complete the mission, providing no grounds for treason. Leave a third of the exiles in Sippar; take your second group down the western tributary to Nippur; and make your final deposit in Erech. But do it quickly, and get out of Babylon before they have a chance to send assassins." Meshach shoved away his plate and wiped his fingers on his robe. "Word about the exiles' arrival hasn't spread yet. I suggest we work out the details for Sippar so you can be on your way to Nippur right away. You made good time from Rezeph—remarkable, really, considering the number of exiles in your train—but you must continue to travel quickly, before General Nebuzaradan bands together with the remainder of his army in Babylon."

I lifted my goblet for the servant to refill—unable to keep my hand from shaking this time.

CHAPTER 27

MERARI

"Babylon, the jewel of kingdoms, the pride and glory of the
Babylonians, will be overthrown by God like Sodom and Gomorrah."
-Isaiah 13:19

 eshach invited Helah and me to remain in his villa during the two days he and Idan worked to place the exiles in Sippar. Our time there was a gift. His household servants, all Judean exiles, educated us on the culture, history, food, and dress of our new land. The governor even gave Helah and me each a new pair of sandals on the morning of our departure. He helped us into his fine carriage. The driver, Jehoshaphat, followed the governor's gilded palanquin to the docks, where we would embark on the rest of our journey.

The carriage stopped on the docks, and Jehoshaphat offered his hand to steady us down, but I was too overwhelmed by the sights, smells, and sounds on the docks. I stood in the carriage, gawking at our Scythian caravan—now missing a third of our captive friends. The reality hit me like a brick.

I clutched Jehoshaphat's hand. "Where have they taken everyone?"

He leaned close, speaking only for Helah and me to hear. "Every exile serves in a business, home, or temple. If they prove exceptional in some talent or knowledge, they're educated and promoted."

"Come, Merari!" Idan shouted, waving at us to hurry.

Jehoshaphat patted my hand and extracted his from my grip. "They'll adjust, Mistress Merari. We all do. Yahweh is good in Babylon."

His confident smile coaxed me from the carriage, and Helah followed close behind. *Yahweh is good in Babylon.* The words did little to console me.

As we approached Idan and Azat, Meshach gave instructions. "I'm sending my steward, Jehoshaphat, to be your guide for the journey. He's more trustworthy than any Babylonian you'll encounter, and he's often taken me down the tributaries to visit Shadrach and Abednego." I noticed surprise on Jehoshaphat's face, but the older man winked at me, seeming unperturbed. I was relieved to have him with us.

Near the river, dock hands loaded supplies and humans on large, round vessels, woven of reed and covered in black pitch. How could they carry horses and wagons full of gold? I tapped Jehoshaphat's shoulder. "Those don't look particularly sturdy. How many will we need to carry our whole caravan?"

"Are you our new commander?" Idan shouted at me over the dock chaos. "Get on the first *quffa* with Jehoshaphat and wait."

Meshach's steward bowed and nudged both Helah and me toward the first boat. He whispered as we walked. "Don't worry, Mistress Merari. The *quffas* are very safe and can carry a dozen humans—or six of the Scythians with their horses." Helah and I stepped onto the first rocking vessel, joining Idan and Azat's stallions and four more warriors with their horses. My fingernails dug into the reed side-rail when Idan and Azat joined us, rocking us mercilessly.

"Get us out of here, Jehoshaphat." Idan watched over his shoulder, but the caravan kept growing longer with more quffas, too long to see the end. He finally faced forward with a sigh. "I've given them ram's horns to blow if there's trouble at the rear."

Jehoshaphat navigated the tributary split masterfully, heading west. He earned more than his weight in gold when he alerted Idan to a quffa's wrong turn—one carrying a wagon full of gold. Another quffa pilot docked so the Scythians could recover the wagon—and kill the thieving quffa pilot. A horseman on land caught up to shout that the wagon was recovered and sailing again, allowing Idan to relax and the rest of us to enjoy a peaceful sail until well after midday.

We stopped near a small village to refresh ourselves. Jehoshaphat expertly sailed the vessel into the shallows so we could debark without a dock. "Babylon is around the bend, Commander."

Idan merely nodded, his jaw flexed. Without delay, we were back on the river, sailing past the glory and splendor of Babylon. Both frightening and intriguing, the capital made me want to flee, yet drew me. Not for its wealth or splendor but because I longed to run through its streets calling Elon's name.

Azat laid his hand over mine on the rail, deep creases on his brow. "You love him still?"

I placed my other hand over his, securing his friendship, not wanting to hurt him. "Elon was my first love. The father of my only child. I'll always love him." He nodded and watched Babylon grow smaller behind us. I watched, too, now anxious to forget it. "I'm a simple woman, Azat. I want only to love a family, to live in community, and to serve Yahweh with all my heart."

He placed his second hand atop mine, our pile now four-hands tall, and then searched my eyes. "If that's true, Merari, then we're not so different after all."

I swallowed the lump rising in my throat and gently pulled my hands away. He brushed my cheek and moved over to talk with Idan. Closing my eyes, I repeated my husband's name to focus my wandering heart.

Meshach had said some Jewish artisans actually thrived in Babylon. *Two days, and I could be reunited with my husband.* It was the thought that sustained me through the first night's camp and the second day's sail. Every time Azat's glances unsettled me, I focused on the countryside and tried harder to remember Elon's face.

By the time we docked at Nippur, I rushed off the quffa and dragged Helah with me onto the dock.

A large man in a dirty robe walked toward me. "That's a lovely harp you have there."

Suddenly, Azat stood between us like a shield. "We're looking for Governor Shadrach." He bowed, scooting me aside and making room for Idan who was hurrying our direction.

The stranger assessed the endless line of quffas, concern lifting his brows. "I'm Shadrach. Your cargo appears to be Jews. I knew the siege on Jerusalem had ended. Are these the only exiles that survived?"

"No. We left a thousand with the king in Rezeph and six hundred and fifty with your brother in Sippar. We'll divide the remaining captives between Nippur and Erech."

The governor visibly relaxed. "Good. Good. We're an agricultural city as you can see." He held his arms out, showcasing his straw- and dirt-covered robe. "Please, come to my villa this evening for a meal. You can tell me if Meshach still wears his extravagant robes. We'll plan to place six hundred and fifty exiles after the sesame harvest is complete. Until then, your men can rest and enjoy the peace and quiet of Nippur."

He offered his hand to Idan but the commander exchanged an awkward glance with Azat, leaving the governor's hand hanging. "Your brother and the prophet Ezekiel have warned me to hurry to Erech."

"Ezekiel?" Shadrach's hand fell, and a lopsided grin chased away all offense. "A Scythian prince listens to Yahweh's prophet?"

Crimson splotches bloomed on Idan's neck. He dropped his gaze, scuffed his leather boot on the dock. "I saw proof."

"Then listen well, my friend." He extended his hand again. "Debark only the six hundred and fifty who are to remain in Nippur and be on your way."

Startled by the urgency, I blurted, "Wait! I need to find Elon."

"Elon?" The governor looked to Idan first but then nodded permission for me to explain.

"Elon is my husband, a harp maker from Jerusalem, taken in the exile eleven years ago."

Pity replaced his curiosity, and nausea swept over me. "I'm sorry. We have no harp makers in Nippur." He swiped dirt and straw from his rough-spun robe. "You should hurry to Erech. Abednego has more artists than soldiers."

I smiled politely and bowed, not trusting my voice to offer gratitude. Helah's arm came around me, guiding me to shore. Azat paused her departure, whispering something. We stayed near the docks, eating a quick meal from the supplies we'd purchased at Sippar. I wasn't hungry.

"Merari, you must eat something." Helah shoved a piece of bread at me. "Azat said it will be three more days of sailing to Erech. You can't travel on an empty stomach."

I took the bread and forced my greatest fear into words. "What if Elon isn't in Erech? What then?"

"Then you trust Yahweh's plan for you."

Her response jolted me from melancholy, and I could only gawk.

"What?" she said, defensive, as if she talked of Yahweh all the time. "I can hardly deny a God who saved my life, healed Azat, and speaks to Scythians, can I?" She hurried to her feet. "Eat your bread and let's say good-bye to our friends."

I took a bite and watched her embrace the debarking exiles. Remembering the bitter woman she was, I praised Yahweh for the friend she'd become, and my spirit brightened. *Yahweh, please give me Helah's faith—to trust in Your plan for me—no matter what I find in Erech.*

CHAPTER 28

IDAN

*"Therefore this is what the Sovereign L*ORD *says:*
'Woe to the city of bloodshed! I, too, will pile the wood high.
So heap on the wood and kindle the fire.
Cook the meat well, mixing in the spices; and let the bones be
charred.'"
-Ezekiel 24:9–10

*G*overnor Shadrach ordered enough food transferred from Nippur's markets to the docks so my men could purchase supplies quickly and get underway by midafternoon. The quffa pilots were expert on the river, so we sailed into the night—but even skilled sailors needed rest.

Progress felt painfully slow and hard to measure as even small villages grew sparse as we sailed farther south. Shore-lines became an indistinguishable blur of grass and trees. Three days on the river and two short overnights on shore under stick-built shelters was grueling. Worse, however, was watching Azat and Merari battle their fear, their love, and the unknown.

When we finally reached Babylon's southernmost city, Merari didn't rush off the quffa as she'd done in Nippur. "Helah and I will wait until you've unloaded the supplies and horses." She gripped the rail like she was chained to it.

While Azat and Yermek coordinated the debarking, I spotted a significant contingent of horsemen riding out from the city. Pointing, I asked Jehoshaphat, "Should I assume that's Governor Abednego, or alert my archers?"

A smile overshadowed his weariness. "It's Governor Meshach's twin."

"Twin?" I'd never met twin brothers. "Are they identical?"

Jehoshaphat laughed while unloading more supplies. "Governor Abednego is smaller in stature but has a bigger presence. He reminds me of your captain."

A Jewish Azat. I smiled at the thought but sobered as the horsemen drew nearer, wondering when I'd face the prophet Ezekiel. Meshach said he lived in a small village not far from Erech but often visited Abednego. Would he somehow know I was coming and meet us here, or would Jehoshaphat know the way and perhaps take me to the prophet tomorrow while my men rested?

The governor's contingent skidded to a halt, ten men on fine horses. Abednego and his deputy dismounted, and I immediately understood Jehoshaphat's comment.

"Greetings, Scythians!" The governor waved, walking two steps ahead of a gray-haired, distinguished man dressed in similar royal attire.

I raised my hand in greeting about the time Azat appeared at my right side, the women following close behind. Azat spoke low without moving his lips. "He seems a happy fellow."

The governor halted less than a pace in front of me, backing me up a step. "Our city always welcomes more citizens." He raised on tiptoes, looking over my shoulder, and shot a panicked glance at the sober, middle-aged man beside him. "Are these the exiles?"

The older man nodded but was focused on me. "And you are Prince Idanthyrsus."

My blood ran cold. Few in Babylon knew my full name. "Who are you?" But I already knew.

He looked through me, speaking as if reading an invisible scroll. *"On the nineteenth day of Tebeth, you laid siege to Jerusalem. When you broke through the walls, you found a city of bloodshed before a sword was drawn—a cooking pot full of bones."*

My knees felt like water, memories pounding my head like a hammer. "Stop!" I cried, stumbling back into Merari. I glimpsed the eyes of the woman I'd found that day, revisiting the haunting images in her home. The pot of charred bones, the horrors beyond warfare. Azat steadied me.

Merari placed her hand on my cheek. "You kept me safe, Idan. You saved my life."

How could she look at me with such kindness? After what she'd suffered? After all the blood I'd shed in my life. I looked at the borrowed harp tucked under her arm and groaned. "You have no idea what I've done."

A gentle hand rested on my shoulder and drew my attention. "My name is Ezekiel, Commander. Yahweh has gone to a lot of trouble to bring you here." He then raised his voice, addressing my troops. "Prince Idan will have an announcement for you shortly. Make camp within our city walls. You'll find fresh straw for your horses and barracks for the men. All women will stay in the governor's guest house. We've prepared for your arrival for seven years. You're all welcome here." He turned to Azat, Helah, and Merari. "You're all welcome to join us for a meal. We have much to discuss."

Abednego secured a carriage for the two women, while Azat and I started toward our stallions. Ezekiel tapped my shoulder and pointed to my supply donkey on a quffa that had just pulled into the dock. "You should bring the item you've hidden in that saddlebag since you took it from Jerusalem."

Another bolt of shock stole my breath. Azat's eyes nearly popped out of his head. The prophet mounted his horse and Azat followed the governor's contingent into the city, while I hurried to the dock to retrieve the magnificent harp from its hiding place. On my way into the city, I glanced over my shoulder and watched my whole caravan obey this prophet's instructions as if he were their commander. Were they driven by the same wonder and fear I felt?

The city of Erech was much like Sippar and Nippur, its lush green vegetation foreshadowing the market stalls overflowing with fresh fruits and vegetables. Life and laughter filled the streets. Children played with sticks, old women huddled to gossip, and young men viewed us with suspicion as we followed their leaders to the three-story brick home built into the city wall.

I caught up with the others in the governor's courtyard. Abednego and Ezekiel talked quietly together, while Helah and Azat followed, arguing over something. Merari lagged behind, and I realized her whole body trembled.

A sudden wave of pity overwhelmed me. I tucked the hidden treasure under my left arm and wrapped Merari's shoulder with my right. "We'll ask about Elon right away."

She nodded, keeping eyes forward. The fact that she didn't resist my comfort was proof of her despair. What if she didn't find her husband? What if she did? Either way, I should have returned her harp long ago.

We paraded through a courtyard, a long hall, a library, and

finally into a grand banquet hall. Abednego invited us to sit around a rectangular table in a private corner. "Ezekiel, please sit at the head of the table." He sat at the prophet's right and placed me on Ezekiel's left. Azat sat beside me and the women across from us.

Before the food was served, the prophet pinned me with a stare. "Have you any news on the prophet Jeremiah? His correspondence stopped over a year ago. I hoped for word from the Lord, but . . ." He shrugged, his forehead lined with dread.

Why had Yahweh told Ezekiel everything about me and nothing of Jeremiah? The Jerusalem harp scorched my conscience, and I realized there were two treasures I'd kept from Merari. "According to General Nebuzaradan's reports, Jeremiah was taken to Egypt after Nebuchadnezzar's appointed governor of Jerusalem was assassinated. Despite Babylon's best efforts to capture him for his power to bless, your god freed him from Jerusalem's chaos."

A guilty glance at Merari affirmed the betrayal he'd dreaded.

"Praise be to the God of Heaven!" Ezekiel clasped Abednego's shoulder, and the two men congratulated each other and their god for the victory. "Let's thank Him now for our food. I'm sure you must be hungry."

Folding his hands, he began. *"Hear, O Israel: The Lord our God, the Lord is one."* Abednego and Merari joined him in some sort of recitation. *"Love the Lord your God with all your heart and with all your soul and with all your strength. These commandments that I give you today are to be on your hearts. Let it be so."* The three smiled at each other as if joined in a secret pact.

Ezekiel's hard lines softened as he studied Merari, her borrowed harp still tucked beneath her arm. "What is your name, little one?"

"I am Merari, Master Ezekiel. I've come in search of my husband, who was taken captive from Jerusalem in the exile eleven years ago. His name is Elon, and he is—"

"The best harp maker in the world," Ezekiel concluded. "Of course, we knew Elon well."

Shock brightened Merari's eyes, but only for a moment. "You *knew* him?"

The prophet extended his hand to her, as realization stole the color from Merari's cheeks. Abednego wrapped his arm around her shoulders, speaking softly. "Elon died three months ago with a cough and high fever."

"Three months?" She spoke in a whisper.

"But our city is full of his harps and musicians who play them." He glanced at Ezekiel, almost panicked. A plea.

Merari dropped her gaze, studying her hands as if a new discovery. "I have no one left." Her voice was small, childlike, wrenching my heart.

The prophet exchanged a wary glance with our host. "That's not exactly true, Merari." Ezekiel waited until she met his gaze. "Since you prayed the Shema with us, I assume you were faithful to Yahweh—as was Elon."

"Yes, of course."

"Then you likely knew of Jeremiah's prophecies that the exiles were to build houses, plant fields, and . . . marry. We have few visitors in Erech, since we're the southernmost city in Babylon, so most of those who left spouses in Jerusalem gave up hope of ever seeing them again." He paused a heartbeat, inhaled a deep breath, and closed his eyes. "Elon left a widow and three sons, my dear."

CHAPTER 29

MERARI

*"This is what the L*ORD *Almighty, the God of Israel,*
says to all those I carried into exile from Jerusalem to Babylon:
'Build houses and settle down; plant gardens and eat what they
produce.
Marry and have sons and daughters . . . Increase in number there; do
not decrease.'"
-Jeremiah 29:4–6

*J*heard Helah's gasp and felt the news of my husband's marriage like another rock on my grave. I felt sadness but not betrayal. How could he have imagined Yahweh would bring me to this place? I had grieved him for eleven years. Now I grieved for the completeness of my losses. Everything that was once Merari was gone. I had no family. No home. No legacy. Even Jeremiah was a world away. I was alone in this world and would live out my days in exile. A yawning void opened in my chest, stealing my very essence.

"Merari, come." Helah was on her feet, speaking to the

governor. "She needs rest. If you'll tell me where the women are staying—"

"Bring her this way." The governor, too, hurried to his feet. Both lifting me and leading me away. "You will both stay in one of my guest chambers," he said.

I followed down a hallway, lined with colorful, patterned tapestries. Our sandals clicked on tiled floors, and a cool evening breeze stirred through the tall, narrow windows. For the first time, I wondered what my future held. Without a husband, I would be sold as a slave or married to a man I didn't know. The thought tipped the boiling pot of my emotions, and I covered my first sob. I don't remember entering the chamber or Abednego's departure, only curling into a ball on a soft mattress and crying myself to sleep.

In the darkness, I huddled over a steaming bowl of lamb stew and heard the chilling sound of a jackal's growl—and woke to Helah's snoring.

An amethyst glow shone through the latticed window of an elegant chamber. I slipped out of bed, pushed open the lattice, and surveyed the city from my third-story perch. Multileveled, brick buildings spread out like a great sea. Erech was larger than Jerusalem. Streets fanned out like spokes on a wheel from a central ziggurat, and I felt a chill, wondering if Yahweh's faithful had fallen into idolatry even in their exile.

"It's a beautiful city."

I gasped, whirling to find Idan seated on a cushion in the corner, his face lined with sleeplessness. "What are you doing here?"

"Helah said I could stay to give you this." He held the borrowed harp King Nebuchadnezzar had given me.

"Thank you. You can leave it." I turned back around to look out the window.

"That's not all." I looked over my shoulder, and he lifted a wrapped bundle that I'd seen strapped to his saddlebag for the duration of our journey.

"What is it?"

"I said you could stay if you didn't wake her." Helah groused from the mattress, stretching and yawning.

"I didn't wake her. I woke you. Go get something to break your fast."

Helah scooted off the bed. "I refuse to leave you two alone. It's not—"

"Go. Now." Idan's threatening glare sent her out the door, but he fell silent, the bundle still in his hands.

With emotions still tight as a harp string, I couldn't stand it. "Either give it to me or leave."

He dropped his head, and I regretted my harshness. Walking over to the bed, he laid the bundle down and removed the dirty cloth.

Even in the dim light, I knew what it was. The streaks of dark and light in the polished olive-wood harp glimmered in dawn's glow. I covered my mouth with a trembling hand and ran my fingers over the inlaid ivory and lapis, memories flooding in. "Elon played this for me on our wedding night to calm me." I swept my fingers over the strings, the sound rich and deep. "He played it every night until he was taken captive, and I played it for our son every night until . . ."

Idan went to one knee beside me. "Merari, please forgive me. I should have given it to you long ago."

I reached for it with trembling hands and placed it in my lap. Eyes closed, I tried to lose myself in the music. The sound was familiar, but the feel was now foreign. Opening my eyes, I pointed at my borrowed harp in the corner. "*That* is my harp, Idan. This one is Elon's." My heart knew the action I must take, but my will cried against it. *Why must I give up my last memory of him, Yahweh?*

You will always have your memories, but your hands must be empty to embrace new treasure.

My eyes shot open. "Did you say that?"

Idan looked as startled as I felt. "Say what?"

Heart fluttering, I knew I'd heard Yahweh's voice.

Idan reached for my hand, eyes wide. "What did you hear?" He knew it too.

"This treasure belongs to Elon's widow, Idan. Will you give it to her?" I laid it aside and brushed his cheek. "Yahweh offers new treasures for me."

"What treasures?" Azat stood beside Helah in the doorway, eyes focused on Idan and his hand holding mine.

Both he and Helah carried trays of food. Azat took four steps toward the bed and slammed his tray on a table. Nudging Idan and the harp aside, he leaned over me, a handbreadth from my face. "You and Yahweh are my treasures. Embrace me, Merari."

I could barely breathe, and then I realized . . . "Where is your crutch?" He'd crossed the chamber without it.

"Marry me." He didn't flinch.

A thousand questions assaulted me, but only one truly mattered. "If I return with you to Scythia, you'll be killed for worshiping Yahweh."

"He's not returning to Scythia." Idan stood next to him, grinning. "He's remaining in Erech as the governor's new bodyguard."

Astounded, I met Azat's intensity once more. "Marry me, Merari."

This time, I saw the hint of a grin on his handsome features, and my heart fluttered, not from fear but with certainty that Yahweh had done a great work after I left Abed-nego's table last night. I cradled his face in my hands. "With the approval of Erech's elders, I will marry you, my friend." I brushed a kiss across his lips and felt a tingle to the tips of my toes.

"That's enough of that!" Helah bustled across the room, tray in hand. "Out. Men out. If we're to have the wedding today, there's a lot of planning—"

"Today?"

Azat kissed the tip of my nose. "So you can't change your mind."

CHAPTER 30

"Yet in the towns of Judah and the streets of Jerusalem that are
deserted,
inhabited by neither people nor animals, there will be heard
once more
the sounds of joy and gladness, the voices of bride and bridegroom,
and the voices of those who bring thank offerings to the house of the
Lord, saying,
'Give thanks to the Lord Almighty, for the Lord is good; his love
endures forever.'"
-Jeremiah 33:10–11

The moment Idan and Azat left my chamber this morning, six giggling handmaids descended on me, creating a woman I barely recognized in the polished-bronze mirror I now held in my hand. A single brazier gave us warmth and light now that the sun had set. Had I ever lived a whole day without doing any work at all?

On the day I married Elon, my family had much to prepare for the wedding feast and little wealth to cover such an extravagance. My wedding garment was a new but sensible woolen robe with a crown of wildflowers to hold my veil in place. I'd barely finished helping bake the last loaves of bread when we heard the bridegroom's march; Elon's rich, bass voice leading his friends to my parents' home to collect his bride. I had been utterly content, fulfilled, and happy with the one my heart adored.

Tonight, I felt like a queen. My fingers strummed the gemstones dangling before my eyes, each one secured with a silver chain to an elegant silver headpiece. "Helah, I can't accept this extravagant gift from Ezekiel."

"You can and you will." She tied the last of my pearls into my braid, these from Abednego. "Ezekiel and the governor are your family now. These gifts serve as your dowry."

Hearing the tremor in her voice, I sniffed back tears for fear of smudging my kohl-rimmed eyes.

"There," she said, securing the last braid with a leather tie. "Beautiful."

The maids painting my feet with henna stepped away. "We're finished, too," one of them proclaimed.

I rose from my cushions on unsteady feet, stretching arms and back after the long day of sitting. All seven women huddled behind me, and an awkward silence crept into the room. I turned to find them all staring. Weeping with beaming smiles.

Helah rushed to embrace me. "Your groom will think he's marrying a dream."

As if summoned by their words, lively strains of the bridegroom's processional whispered on the night breeze. My heart skipped as my eyes met Helah's.

Delighted squeals filled my chamber. "The bridegroom comes!" Seven women scurried to last-minute tasks, more frenzied than hens when a fox is stalking. "Get her veil. Hurry!" Four of them, one on each corner of a tapestry-weight, colorful cloth, lifted it above my head and centered it over me, letting it fall to cover my hair, jewels, and the lovely makeup they'd spent all afternoon applying. I chuckled at our silly traditions, thankful no one could see.

Helah pressed her lips against my ear. "Listen for the music, Merari. It will become a cacophony outside your door. You'll feel as if your heart might burst with anticipation, and then silence will tip you over the edge. The sound that follows is more glorious than your harp playing." She cradled my head in her hands and kissed me through the cloth as the room fell silent. Had she forgotten I'd been married before?

But as the processional drew near, every word of Helah's description came to life. The intensifying music, the joyous celebration ever building and then halting abruptly outside the door. I held my breath. The knock.

"I've come to claim my bride!" There it was. My bridegroom's voice. And it was, indeed, more glorious than any harp.

"Your bride has made herself ready," Helah answered.

I sat on a cushion, my back to the door. The veil obscured all of me except the cushion and my trembling hands clasped in my lap. Footsteps shuffled out, but only one pair of sandals drew near. Jeweled, with familiar feet in them.

Azat knelt before me and slowly, timidly, rolled up the veil that separated us. His hands trembled as violently as mine, but his face lit with wonder when he saw me.

"You are mine," he whispered.

Covering a laugh, I cupped his face. "Yes, and we are Yahweh's."

He held my gaze for an excruciating moment, then let his

eyes travel to my lips. Time stood still. My breathing grew ragged. *Kiss me, or I'll die.* He leaned in.

"None of that until after the ceremony." Helah appeared beside him, and I jumped like a child caught stealing dates.

Azat chuckled and whispered, "I should have had Idan keep her in the hall." He tapped my nose and lowered my veil. "Let's get to the ceremony, then." He exited my chamber to the congratulatory cheers of his friends, having confirmed the identity of his bride—a tradition necessitated by our patriarch Jacob's ancient deception, when he was tricked into marrying the wrong sister.

Helah helped me to my feet, and a man's hand cradled mine. "It is my honor to serve as your abba on this special day, Merari." Ezekiel kissed my hand, and my heart melted.

"I am the one most blessed, Lord Ezekiel." The prophet and Helah volunteered to perform the parental rites of the ceremony since I had no living relatives. In many ways, their presence felt every bit as warm and secure as family joined by blood. When hearts are woven together by faith and tears, the love is everlasting and the bonds stronger than iron.

As we neared the banquet hall, I heard a choir of harp players and squeezed Ezekiel's arm, certain they were another gift from him. "The music is lovely. How many harps are playing?"

A slight hesitation before he answered made me curse the blinding veil. "Several, my dear. But this surprise we should let your husband *unveil.*" His word choice was witty but annoying. I fell silent, trying not to pout on my wedding night. It was a simple question. Why couldn't he at least describe the musicians?

The music changed to a familiar bride's song, its familiar words ringing in my mind. *"Listen, daughter, and pay careful attention: Forget your people and your father's house."* The growing clamor of Scythian whispers carried me to my groom. Tonight, I would relinquish my claim as God's chosen. My children would be considered mixed-blood, never worthy to return with the exiles to Jerusalem when Jeremiah's prophecy of seventy years of captivity was fulfilled.

A seed of panic bloomed in my chest as Abednego's voice commenced the ceremony. "We have gathered tonight under this wedding canopy to remember Yahweh's promises to Abraham. First, that his descendants would be as numerous as the stars; and second, that Abraham would bring Yahweh's blessing to *all* nations as we have witnessed this day with our Scythian brothers."

One of the warriors released a jubilant howl, setting off the whole regiment—including Azat and Idan—and it spread to thousands outside the governor's villa. What had happened while I'd been bathed, lotioned, and bejeweled in my chamber? Without seeing anyone's face, I could only hold my breath. Would Ezekiel condemn this behavior at a wedding? Would Abednego order the Scythians' silence? I had agreed to marry a Scythian. I'd grown accustomed to their strange customs. The tattoos. The loud celebrations. But could the Jews of Erech tolerate them?

Incredibly, I heard Ezekiel chuckle with Abednego as the Scythian shouts faded. "Azat," Abednego began again, "we hold to our traditions loosely in order to honor your brotherhood and the faith you've proven in Yahweh. Merari remains a Child of Abraham and by your solemn vow, you will enter into Abraham's covenant of circumcision after your wedding week, giving you equal rights and responsibilities with all Yahweh's chosen. Would you like to present your gift to the bride now before we continue with the ceremony?"

"I would indeed, Governor." Ezekiel left my side, and without warning, Azat lifted off my veil, handing it to a stunned Helah. He brushed my cheek, and led me by the hand. "I'd like to introduce you to our musicians."

Weaving past the canopy and around the private table where we'd eaten last night's meal, I saw ten musicians tucked away in the banquet hall's corner. Six men, one woman, and three boys—one, no older than ten; and the others twins, perhaps seven years old. I knew them without an introduction. All three boys looked like my son, Neriah.

I covered a gasp and stared at Elon's harp in the woman's arms.

Azat wrapped his strong arm around my shoulder and whispered against my ear, "Abednego summoned Elon's widow and sons to the villa to present Elon's harp. She was overwhelmed by your sacrifice and offered to gather her friends to play for our wedding." He kissed my forehead and turned to the musicians. "My friends, this is Merari, Elon's first wife and a skilled harp maker." He extended his hand toward the woman. "Merari, this is Mistress Selah and her three sons: Ethan, Mahli, and Malluk."

All four stood and we bowed to each other in greeting. Selah took my hand, her eyes overflowing with emotion. "Your kindness in giving me a harp my husband—*our* husband— made *in* Jerusalem is a great treasure." She turned then to Azat, including both of us in her next words. "I realize life in Erech will be very different for you both, and perhaps you can't give me an answer now . . ."

Dread rose prickly flesh on my arms, and I reached for Azat's hand, preparing for the worst. What might she ask?

"My sons and I would consider it a great honor if you, Merari, could teach them their abba's skill of harp making.

Elon hadn't trained an apprentice, and his death was so unexpect—"

I pulled her into a hug, my heart aching at her loss. But I felt certain teaching Elon's sons to carry on his trade would begin the healing—and provide steady income for these boys to care for their ima. I looked over her shoulder to gain my new husband's permission.

His nod was all I needed. "It would be my privilege, Selah. We'll begin after the wedding festivities."

Azat offered his hand. "I have a gift for Idan before I'm officially wed and become Abednego's guard."

He led me back to the *chuppah*, where I now saw all the attendants standing. Four Scythians held the poles of the canopy, while Abednego stood beneath it waiting with Idan. Ezekiel and Helah stood side by side at the edge of the covering, ready to offer the daughter of their hearts.

Yermek stood in the shadows but approached with a wrapped bundle when we neared the canopy, offering it to Azat. "Thank you, Captain Yermek." My groom placed his fist over his heart. "You'll lead my men well."

The baby-faced captain saluted and bowed, stepping back as Azat turned his attention to his commander and friend. His lips quivered, failing many times to speak. I reached for his hand, and he inhaled deeply, lifting it to his lips and then releasing it. A silent reminder I couldn't help him through this. He must give his heart completely to his friend one last time.

Lifting his gaze to the mountainous man standing three heads taller, he spoke quietly but with utter confidence. "I leave you in good hands, my brother. Yahweh is with you and is returning you to Scythia with a qualified captain, a regiment that would die for you, and three thousand warriors who, because of Ezekiel's prophecies fulfilled before their eyes, now believe He is real." Shouting now to the regiment who stood as witnesses to our ceremony, Azat unwrapped the bundle Yermek delivered—the most beautifully carved mouth harp I'd ever seen. "Idan, to show their devotion—to you and to Yahweh—one of our men carved this harp from a piece of olive wood he brought from Jerusalem. They will stand with you in Scythia, my friend."

Idan's features twisted with emotion, and he covered his face to regain control. Unable to do so, he lifted his hands and shouted his praise to Yahweh in an ear-splitting cry that rattled the stars. Every voice in the room joined him, Jew and Scythian, captive and free.

I wrapped my arms around my husband's neck. "Yahweh has healed us. He has freed the captives, given comfort when we grieved, and anointed us with joy instead of mourning. You, Azat, have been His instrument of healing to me." I brushed a kiss across his lips, smiling into sparkling eyes.

"And you, my love, have shown me the One True God." He shook his head, daunted. "I have so much to learn."

Ezekiel drew us back to the wedding canopy. "We'll learn together—*after* the wedding."

With lifted hands, Abednego quieted the raucous worshipers but only for a time. Our ceremony was short but the most beautiful I recall, and the feast afterward is a legend in Erech's history. The marriage has been even better.

Impossible, you say, for a Jewess and Scythian to dwell in harmony for a lifetime? I say you're right, *but God . . .*

AUTHOR'S NOTE

I hope you've enjoyed Merari's fictional story, and though Idanthyrsus was an actual Scythian king from the sixth century BC, his participation with King Nebuchadnezzar's troops in the destruction of Judah was also fictional.

Why would I build a biblical novel on two fictional characters? Because when I read this verse from Jeremiah, my research led me to the very real possibility of Scythia's involvement.

This is what the Lord says: "Look, an army is coming from the land of the north; a great nation is being stirred up from the ends of the earth. They are armed with bow and spear; they are cruel and show no mercy. They sound like the roaring sea as they ride on their horses; they come like men in battle formation to attack you, Daughter Zion" (6:22–23).

Scythia's history is fascinating but difficult to piece together. Here are a few insights that helped me choose Idan as the main character:

- Scythians were legendary warriors, known for their cruelty, horsemanship, archery skills, and war cries.
- Scythians had a singular passion and devotion to their national gods. Anyone found worshiping a foreign god—even the king's brother—was put to death. What a perfect culture to understand and mete out Yahweh's judgment on the people of Judah, who had worshiped foreign gods for centuries.
- Historical records conflict as to the story of Anacharsis, a Scythian who tried to incorporate Greek worship into his culture's pantheon. Some sources say Idanthyrsus was his brother and the one who killed him for his blasphemy. Others say Idanthyrsus was his nephew, and it was Anacharsis' brother, King Saulius (Idan's father), who killed his brother. When resources conflict, I get to choose details that fit my story line—as did Idan's inner struggle of obedience to his father's command against the inner niggling of conscience and Yahweh's conviction.
- I found more conflicting accounts while trying to describe the appearance of sixth century BC Scythians. Because they were a nomadic culture, without permanent homes or temples, physical representations of their features—hair and eye color—are difficult to ascertain. Archaeologists have discovered from burial sites that some had flattened cheekbones, likely due to lifelong use of a bow. Some resources said they looked like fair-haired Siberians; others said Asian in appearance. All attested to the complete covering of tattoos and an affinity for alcoholic drink and marijuana. (See the following

article for more information on Scythia:
http://bit.ly/2Myhktl)

- My final research discovery came as a complete "accident." I Googled "ancient Jewish harp" in hopes of discovering more about how Merari might have constructed her harps. Instead, articles on *Jew's harps* popped up—the mouth harps Idan and his soldiers play. Of particular interest to me was the ancient *Scythian* mouth harp discovered in the area where Idan and his tribe would have lived. (See the article here: http://bit.ly/2JIyGG7)

I chose to write the story of Psalm 137 because it helps fill in details of Jerusalem's destruction that my full-length novel on Daniel's life couldn't cover. *Of Fire and Lions* releases February 2019 (Waterbrook/Multnomah, Division of Penguin Random House Publishing) and begins with Daniel's captivity (605 BC). The epic tale scans the spectrum of Daniel's life and Judah's reformation in Babylon, culminating at the end of Jeremiah's prophesied seventy years when the exiled remnant returns to Jerusalem. Experience the wonder of Yahweh, the God who controls the power *Of Fire and Lions*.

BIBLE STUDY FOR PSALM 137

To understand the emotional lament and vengeful outcry of Psalm 137, we must understand the events, the land, and the nations involved. Only hearts crushed completely could ache so deeply. And only our God, who was hurt so deeply, would punish completely—and restore so gloriously. Though sin destroyed and God's wrath poured out, Mercy built an even greater gift on the ruins.

> *"[By the waters of Babylon]*
> *we sat as exiles, mourning our captivity,*
> *and wept with great love for Zion."* (137:1 TPT)

1. Why was Zion (Jerusalem) so important to those who remained faithful to Yahweh? (Leviticus 17:2-4; Deuteronomy 12:5-7)

2. On which piece of Temple furniture did Yahweh choose to manifest His presence? (Exodus 25:22)

3. To glimpse the utter devastation felt by these exiles, we must first absorb the complete *separation* they felt from God. All the "normal" ways of connecting with Him were blocked. Imagine if you could no longer pray or read your Bible. No longer enjoy the fellowship or encouragement of other believers. Consider your current relationship with God and write a line or two about what you would miss most if you were separated from all that is familiar about your worship.

Babylon's geography was very different than Jerusalem's. Only the Jordan River flowed through Israel/Judah, no more than a stream in the dry season. The mighty Euphrates River flowed into Babylon, and Nebuchadnezzar's father had begun a complex system of canals to irrigate the entire province. In Judah, streams only swelled during floods from Mount Hermon's spring thaw. Jerusalem's desert soil—full of rocks and sand—limited crops to olives, grapes, barley, wheat, and a few more, but it was *God's* Land promised to the descendants of Abraham, Isaac, and Jacob. When the exiles arrived in Babylon, they saw plants and trees they'd never seen before, growing from rich, black soil without *any* rocks. No barley. No grapes. No olive trees. Babylon grew sesame plants for oil, poplar (willow) trees beside the rivers and streams, and date palms for wine.

"Our music and mirth were no longer heard, only sadness.

We hung up our harps on the willow trees.
Our captors tormented us, saying, 'Make music for us and
sing one of your happy Zion-songs!'
But how could we sing the song of the Lord
in this foreign wilderness?" (137:2-4 TPT)

4. Gloating soldiers goaded their captives to sing songs of their decimated homeland. With the last tattered shreds of dignity they possessed, the captives refused. Put yourself in the captives' sandals. Why would *you* refuse to sing the songs once heard in Yahweh's Temple?

To a faithful Yahweh worshiper, singing "Zion-songs" in exile would be like *forgetting* Jerusalem. And forgetting Jerusalem would be the same as forgetting Yahweh, since Yahweh and Jerusalem's Temple were synonymous in their minds.

May my hands never make music again
if I ever forget you, O Jerusalem.
May I never be able to sing again if I fail to honor Jerusalem
supremely!" (137:5-6 TPT)

5. What specifically about Jerusalem do you think they are vowing to remember?
   • 2 Chronicles 6:6
   • Psalm 132:13-18
   • Isaiah 44:24-28

• Jeremiah 32:42-44

6. Do you think *remembering* is important to God? Why?
   • Genesis 9:15-16
   • Exodus 12:14
   • Exodus 20:8
   • Leviticus 23

7. What is something that the Lord is asking you to commemorate or remember passionately?

The nation of Edom—whose people were the descendants of Esau, Jacob's twin brother (Gen. 25:19-34)—were among the mercenaries in Babylon's vast army. History tells us Nebuchadnezzar also used Arabs, Persians, Scythians, Medes, and Syrians to destroy God's people.

> *And Lord, may you never forget*
> *what the sons of Edom did to us, saying,*
> *"Let's raze the city of Jerusalem and burn it to the ground!"*
> *Listen, O Babylon, you evil destroyer!*
> *The one who destroys you will be rewarded above all others.*
> *You will be repaid for what you've done to us.*
> *Great honor will come to those who destroy you and your future,*
> *by smashing your infants against the rubble of your own*
> *destruction. (137:7-9)*

8. The Psalmist just vowed to *never forget* Jerusalem. In the

next breath and with equal passion, he asks that Yahweh *never forget* the horrendous things Edom did to God's people and His holy city. Does God need to be reminded? Of course not, but which heroes of faith reminded God of His character and covenants?

- Exodus 32:13-14
- 2 Kings 20:3
- 2 Chronicles 6:42
- Nehemiah 1:8-9
- Psalm 25:6-7

9. Scripture offers many examples of faithful men and women who "remind" God of His promises as part of their prayers. What Bible verse(s) can you incorporate into a prayer that reminds both you and the Lord of His faithfulness? (i.e. Romans 8:28)

10. Jeremiah 1:14-15 makes it clear that it was God who summoned the nations to pour out His wrath on Jerusalem. Why then does God punish Edom, Babylon, and the other nations for destroying His people? (Isaiah 10:12; Obadiah 12-13; Habakkuk 2:4-8)

11. When the nations delighted in vengeance and became arrogant in their role as God's rod of discipline, the Lord turned His wrath on them. Both the Old and New Testaments command us to love our neighbor and pray for our enemies (Lev. 19:17-18; Matt. 5:44). Psalm 83:13-18 is a beautiful prayer expressing both righteous anger and a pure heart. Is there an "enemy" in your life that needs to feel God's tempest —until they seek His face in repentance and confess that He alone is Most High over all the earth? Ultimately, we—like the

Israelites—will witness God's faithfulness to either judge righteously or forgive lavishly.

As for me, I'm forever grateful for His mercy. Without the redeeming Blood of the Lamb, my eternity would be lost with the Babylonian captors. Through the death and resurrection of Jesus Christ, I can come boldly before the Throne of Grace and cry, "Abba!" with full assurance that His dwelling place is within me. (Hebrews 4:16; Galatians 4:6; Romans 8:11)

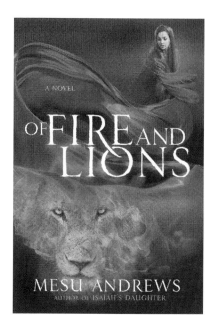

Available on Kindle HERE: https://amzn.to/2Lrv5t4

And in Paperback HERE: https://amzn.to/2L1Goff

The Hunter and the Valley of Death is a profound meditation on life, death, loss, and love. Formatted as a fantasy parable **based on Psalm 23**, this story shows that there is only one who could kill Death, and because of him, and him alone, we say, "**Oh, Death, where is your sting?**"

A man who calls himself Hunter wakes up in the Valley of Death and realizes he's given up everything to attempt to kill Death so that he can bring his Love back to life - but when he fails, who will be there to rescue him?

Each book in *The Psalm Series* comes with an in-depth Bible study of the psalm the story is based on, and an explanation of the

author's approach to the Scripture text. *The Hunter and the Valley of Death* comes with an additional, in-depth explanation of the story's symbolism.

Available in e-book, paperback, and audiobook formats at https://psalmseries.com.

Praetorian Prefect Sextus Burrus spent his life fighting for the glory of Rome, but that glory has lost its shine. As both his health and career crumble, he is drawn toward the seemingly inexhaustible peace of one of his Jewish prisoners, the Apostle Paul, and his friend, the Apostle Timothy.

Finally, an unexpected crisis presses Timothy to reexamine everything, and places all hope for Paul's freedom on the shoulders of Praetorian Prefect Sextus Burrus.

Available at https://psalmseries.com.

ABOUT THE AUTHOR

MESU ANDREWS is the award-winning author of *Love Amid the Ashes* and numerous other novels including *The Pharaoh's Daughter* and *Miriam*. Her deep understanding of–and love for–God's Word brings the biblical world alive for readers. Mesu lives in North Carolina with her husband Roy and enjoys spending time with her growing tribe of grandchildren. Find her at mesuandrews.com.

THE PSALM SERIES BIBLE STUDY

Go to psalmseries.com to download a FREE 7-Day Bible Study based on the psalms.

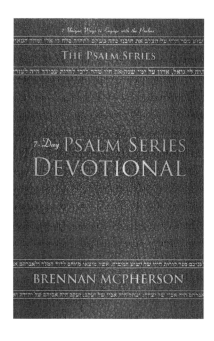

Made in the USA
Coppell, TX
16 January 2020

14594816R00118